THE BOOKS OF
elsewhere
volume one
THE SHADOWS

by Jacqueline West

illustrated by Poly Bernatene

SCHOLASTIC INC.
New York Toronto London Auckland
Sydney Mexico City New Delhi Hong Kong

ISBN 978-0-545-38990-7

 Published by Scholastic Inc., 557 Broadway, New York, NY 10012,
by arrangement with Dial Books for Young Readers, a division of
Penguin Young Readers Group, a member of Penguin Group (USA) Inc.

12 11 10 9 8 7 6 5 4 3 2 1 11 12 13 14 15 16/0

Printed in the U.S.A. 75

First Scholastic printing, September 2011

Designed by Jennifer Kelly
Text set in Requiem

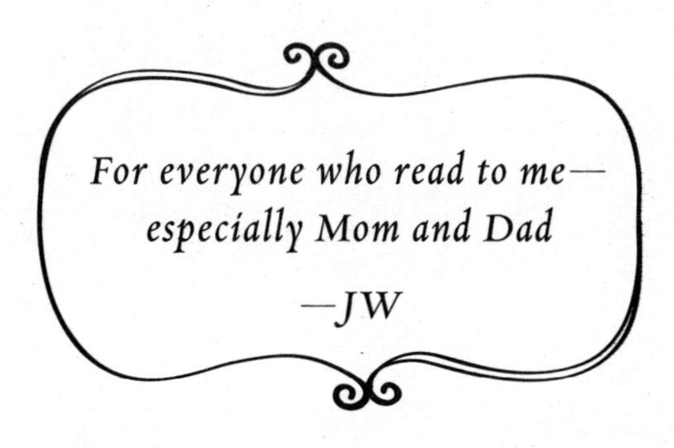

For everyone who read to me—
especially Mom and Dad

—JW

THE BOOKS OF
elsewhere
volume one
THE SHADOWS

MS. MCMARTIN WAS definitely dead. It had taken some time for the neighbors to grow suspicious, since no one ever went in or came out of the old stone house on Linden Street anyway. However, there were several notable clues that things in the McMartin house were not as they should have been. The rusty mailbox began to bulge with odd and exotic mail-order catalogs, which eventually overflowed the gaping aluminum door and spilled out into the street. The gigantic jungle fern that hung from the porch ceiling keeled over for lack of water. Ms. McMartin's three cats, somewhere inside the house, began the most terrible yowling ever heard on quiet old Linden Street. After a few days of listening to *that*, the neighbors had had enough.

The authorities arrived in a big white van. They

marched in a group up the porch steps, knocked at the door, waited for a moment, and then picked the lock with a handy official lock-picking tool. A few minutes went by. All the neighbors held their breath, watching through the gaps in their curtains. Soon the uniformed group reappeared, rolling a white-sheeted stretcher onto the porch. They locked the ancient front door behind them and drove away, stretcher and all.

Rumors soon began to fly regarding where and how Ms. McMartin had finally kicked it. Mrs. Nivens, who had lived next door for as long as anyone could remember, told Mrs. Dewey that it had happened in the hallway, where someone—or *something*—had startled Ms. McMartin so badly that she fell down the stairs. Mr. Fergus told Mr. Butler that Ms. McMartin had collapsed on the living room rug in front of the fireplace, while a sheaf of secret family papers went up in smoke behind the grate. Mr. Hanniman decreed that she had died of old age, plain and simple—he had heard that she was 150 years old, after all. And there were various theories as to just how much of Ms. McMartin's face had been eaten by her cats.

Ms. McMartin had no close family. Her nearest relative was a distant cousin who had recently died in Shanghai, after a severe allergic reaction to a bowl of turtle and arsenic soup. There was no one to come and collect an inheritance, or to dig through the rickety attic for long-lost treasures. The old stone house, covered with encroaching scarves of ivy, was left full of its antique furniture and strange knickknacks. Ms. McMartin's yowling cats were the only items to be removed from the house, wrestled into kitty carriers by three scratched and bleeding animal shelter workers. And then, according to Mrs. Nivens, who saw it all through her kitchen window, just as they were about to be loaded into the animal shelter truck, the three kitty carriers popped open simultaneously. A trio of gigantic cats shot across the lawn like furry cannonballs. The sweaty shelter manager wiped a smudge of blood off his cheek, shrugged, and said to the other two, "Well—how about some lunch?"

It wasn't long before someone heard about the old stone house for sale at an astonishingly low price and decided to buy it.

These someones were a Mr. Alec and Mrs. Alice Dunwoody, a pair of more than slightly dippy mathematicians. The Dunwoodys had a daughter named Olive—but she had nothing to do with the house-buying decision. Olive was eleven, and was generally not given much credit. Her persistently lackluster grades in math had led her parents to believe that she was some kind of genetic aberration—they talked to her patiently, as if she were a foreign exchange student from a country no one had ever heard of.

In late June, Mr. Hambert, Realtor, led the Dunwoodys through the McMartin house. It was a muggy afternoon, but the old stone house was dark and cool inside. Trailing along behind the rest of the group, Olive could feel the little hairs on her bare arms standing up. Mr. Hambert, on the other hand, was sweating like a mug of root beer in the sun. His cheeks were pushed up into two red lumps by his wide smile. He could smell a sale, and it smelled as good as a fresh bacon, lettuce, and tomato sandwich. As they walked along the first-floor hallway, he kept up a flow of chitchat.

"So, how did you two meet?" Mr. Hambert asked Mr. and Mrs. Dunwoody, pulling the chain of a dusty hanging lamp.

"We met in the library at Princeton," answered Mrs. Dunwoody, her eyes glowing with the memory. "We were both reading the same journal—*The Absolutely Unrelenting Seriousness of Mathematics for the New Generation*—"

"Or '*Ausom*'—get it?" interjected Mr. Dunwoody. " 'Awesome.' Very clever."

"—and Alec asked me, 'Have you seen the misprint on page twenty-five?' They had written that Theodorus's Constant—"

"Is the square root of *two*!" interjected Mr. Dunwoody again. "How their copy editors missed that, I can't imagine."

“Oh, we both laughed and laughed,” sighed Mrs. Dunwoody with a misty look at her husband.

“Well, you must be a regular math whiz, with parents like yours—am I right?” said Mr. Hambert, leaning his sweaty face toward Olive.

Mr. Dunwoody patted Olive’s shoulder. “Math isn’t really her thing. Olive is a very . . . *creative* girl, aren’t you, Olive?”

Olive nodded, and looked down at the toes of her sneakers.

Mr. Hambert kept up his shiny-cheeked smile. “Well, good for you,” he said, stopping in front of a pair of dark wood doors, carved into shiny raised squares. He pushed them open with a grand gesture.

“The library,” he announced.

Through the doors was a large, dusty room, almost the size of a small ballroom. The wooden floor was a little scratched, and the tiles around the giant fireplace were chipped here and there, but these flaws made the vast room seem cozier. In fact, it looked as though it might have been used yesterday. Long shelves, still covered with rows of embossed leather volumes, stretched from the hardwood floor to the stenciled ceiling. Ladders on wheels, the kind that Olive had only seen in old paintings, were leaning against the shelves so that the very highest books could be reached. There were hundreds, maybe thousands of books, obviously collected by several generations of McMartins.

"The managers of the estate have decided to sell the contents along with the house. Of course, you can dispose of these however you choose," said Mr. Hambert consolingly, as though so many books would be a terrible bother.

"This room would be just perfect for studying, correcting papers, writing articles . . . don't you think?" said Mrs. Dunwoody to Mr. Dunwoody dreamily.

"Oh, yes, very cozy," agreed Mr. Dunwoody. "You know, I don't believe that we need more time to make up our minds—do you, dear?"

Mr. and Mrs. Dunwoody exchanged another misty look. Then Mr. Dunwoody declared, "We'll take it."

Mr. Hambert's face turned as red as a new potato. He burbled and shone and shook Mr. Dunwoody's hand, then Mrs. Dunwoody's hand, then Mr. Dunwoody's hand again.

"Excellent! Excellent!" he boomed. "Congratulations—perfect house for a family! So big, so full of history . . . A quick look around the second floor, and we can go back to my office and sign the papers!"

They all trooped up the mossy carpet of the staircase, Mr. Hambert in the lead, puffing happily, Mr. and Mrs. Dunwoody following hand in hand, smiling up at the high ceilings as though some lovely algebraic theorem unfolded there. Olive trailed behind, running her hand up the banister and collecting a pile of thick dust. At the top of the stairs, she rolled the dust into a little ball and blew it off of her palm. It floated slowly down, past the banister, past the old wall sconces, into the dark hallway.

Her parents had disappeared into one of the bedrooms. She could still hear Mr. Hambert shouting "Excellent! Excellent!" every now and again.

Olive stood by herself on the landing and felt the big stone house loom around her. *This is our house,* she told herself, just to see how it felt. *Our house.* The words hovered in her mind like candle smoke. Before Olive could quite believe them, they had faded away.

Olive turned in a slow circle. The hall stretched away from her in two directions, dwindling into darkness at both ends. Dim light from one hanging lamp outlined the frames of the pictures on the walls. Behind Olive, at the top of the stairs, was a large painting in a thick gold frame. Olive liked to paint, but she mostly made squiggly designs or imaginary creatures from the books she read. She had never painted anything like this.

Olive peered into the canvas. It was a painting of a forest at night. The twigs of leafless trees made a black web against the sky. A full moon pressed its face through the clouds, touching a path of white stones that led into the dark woods and disappeared. But it seemed to Olive that somewhere—maybe just at the end of that white path, maybe in that darkness where the moonlight couldn't reach—there was something *else* within that painting. Something she could almost see.

"Olive?" Mrs. Dunwoody's head popped through a doorway along the hall. "Don't you want to see your bedroom?"

Olive walked slowly away from the painting, keeping her eye on it over her shoulder. She would figure it out later, she told herself. She would have plenty of time.

THE DUNWOODYS MOVED in two weeks later. Everything had been taken out of their two-bedroom apartment and scattered through the stone mansion on Linden Street. In the big old house, their belongings looked small and out of place, like tiny visitors from outer space trying to blend in at a Victorian ball. The Dunwoodys' expensive computer sat on an old wooden desk in the library, where antique books seemed to look at it a bit distrustfully. There weren't enough outlets in the kitchen for all of their appliances, but in every drawer and corner they found utensils that no one could figure out—they could have been cooking accessories or dental equipment, for all any of the Dunwoodys knew. Sepia portraits hung from the walls, and glass medicine bottles stood in every bathroom cabinet.

In one spare bedroom, Olive discovered an old chest of drawers that was full of handkerchiefs and lacy bloomers, a pair of spectacles, and pearl-buttoned gloves. There were even ropes of fake pearls and colored glass beads that she could try on and pretend to be Cleopatra or Queen Guinevere. Even though Mr. Hambert had said everything in the house was theirs, Olive always carefully wrapped the jewelry and the gloves back up in tissue paper and returned them to the drawers, just as she had found them. It felt right, somehow. It was like being in a museum where you were allowed to play with the exhibits, not just stare at them through the glass.

At the same time, Olive missed their old apartment, where all the beige walls met at perfect ninety-degree angles, where there were no surprising corners, no twisting hallways, no slanted ceilings to bash your forehead against as you climbed out of the bathtub. This new house was always sneaking up on her.

The Dunwoodys had lived in many different apartments, but somehow they all felt the same to Olive. They were all in three-story buildings made of brick, where all the walls were the same color, and all the windows were the same shape, and you could wander into a neighbor's living room (if their door was unlocked) and spend several minutes lying on their couch, which was exactly like your couch, watching their TV, before you realized you were in the wrong place. Olive had done this quite a few times.

No one would ever mistake the big house on Linden Street for someplace else. This house was crumbly and dark and weird. It was full of corners that the lights never reached. It made squeaking, moaning sounds when the wind changed, like a dog howling or a child whimpering. Olive had never been anywhere—not even the doctor's office, not even *gym class*—that made her feel so out of place, or so alone.

And the painting at the top of the stairs still seemed to be keeping a secret. Olive stood in front of it for almost half an hour that first night, until her eyes crossed and bits of the trees popped out at her. Nothing. Nothing but the feeling that there was something not quite right about this painting.

And it wasn't the only one.

There were paintings all over the house that gave her the same funny feeling. Right outside her bedroom door, there was a painting of a rolling field with a row of little houses in the distance. It was evening in the painting, and all the windows in the houses were dark. But the houses didn't look like they were sleeping comfortably, just waiting for sunrise to come and start another day. The houses looked like they were holding their breath. They crouched among the trees and blew out their lights, trying not to be seen. Seen by what? Olive wondered.

On their first night in the house, Mrs. Dunwoody came upstairs to tuck Olive into bed. Olive heard her mother's steps on the squeaky staircase and reluctantly pulled her eyes away from the painting. She scurried into her room and hopped under the blankets, knocking several pillows onto the floor.

"Ready for bed, sweetie?" asked Mrs. Dunwoody, peeking in.

"Yes," said Olive.

"Good girl." Her mother crossed the room and sat down on the edge of Olive's high, creaky bed. "Are you comfy?"

"Mm-hm," answered Olive.

"I know it's going to take some getting used to, sweetie—this new room, and new house, and new everything. But I bet that in just a few days you're going to start to feel at home here. Don't you like having such a big house and big yard to play in?"

"Yeah . . . kind of," said Olive. "I don't know."

"Just give it a little more time. You'll see."

Her mother stood up. The mattress bounced just a little. "See you in the morning," she whispered from the doorway.

"Um—Mom?" said Olive, just as Mrs. Dunwoody

was pulling the door closed. "Something here is . . . There's something . . . bugging me."

"What is it?" asked her mother.

"That painting, right outside my door? It bothers me. It's . . . creepy."

Olive slid back out of bed and padded into the hallway, where her mother stood, frowning up at the painting.

"This one, of the little town?" said Mrs. Dunwoody doubtfully. "What do you think is creepy about it?"

"It looks . . ." Olive whispered, feeling silly. "I think it looks scared. It's like the houses are trying to pretend they're asleep, and stay quiet . . . like something bad is coming."

"Hmmm," said her mother, trying to hide the skeptical look on her face. "Well, why don't we just take it down?"

Mrs. Dunwoody grabbed the sides of the thick wooden frame and pulled. But the painting didn't budge.

"That's funny," she said.

She tried pushing the frame upward, in case the painting was hung on a hook. Still it didn't move.

"This is very strange," Mrs. Dunwoody said.

Bracing her feet on the hallway carpet, Mrs. Dunwoody got a good grip on the bottom corners of the frame and yanked as hard as she could. Olive thought the frame would either crack in half or her mother would lose her hold on it and go flying backward across the hall. But neither thing happened.

"Oof," puffed Mrs. Dunwoody. "It's really stuck. It must be glued to the wall or something . . . or over time, the wallpaper has bonded to the back of the canvas. Maybe if it got wet . . ." Mrs. Dunwoody trailed off, silently calculating various hypotheses.

"Let's worry about it tomorrow. For now," she said, guiding Olive back into the bedroom, "let's get you tucked in again."

Her mother tugged the covers up under Olive's chin and smoothed the wrinkles around her feet. "Where's Hershel?" she asked.

"Right here," said Olive, holding up the worn brown teddy bear.

"Good. He'll protect you," said Mrs. Dunwoody, heading back toward the door. "But I'll leave the hall light on, just in case."

The door clicked shut behind her mother. Olive lay very still, wide-awake, listening to her mother's footsteps fade away down the hall. Then she swung her legs carefully out of bed, making the bedspread rustle as little as possible.

Olive peeped out the door and looked down the hallway in both directions. Her parents were closed inside their bedroom. The hall lamp sent a soft glow over the thick carpet and made the polished wood along the walls glint like brass. She tiptoed out and stood in front of the painting. The row of houses cowered on their twilit street. Olive grabbed the frame. She pulled and pulled and pulled, but the painting wouldn't move. It felt almost like the painting was part of the wall itself.

Olive walked quietly along the hall toward the stairs, looking carefully at the other paintings. They seemed even stranger in the dim light than they had earlier in the day. One showed a big bowl of fruit, but they were fruits Olive had never seen in any grocery store. They were funnily shaped and strangely colored, and a few of them were sliced open to show bright pink or green centers with glistening seeds. Another painting depicted a rocky, treeless hill and a crumbling stone church, far away in the background. She hadn't noticed it before, but when she squinted and leaned very close, Olive thought that she could make out the bumps and crosses of distant gravestones.

Just to check, she yanked on the frame of each painting. None of them budged. She was just reaching the head of the stairs when something to the left caught her eye. In the big painting of the moonlight and the forest, something had changed.

At first Olive thought that the light looked dif-

ferent, as if the painted moon itself had moved. But no—the moon hung just where it had before, behind the leafless trees. It was something about the shadows. Olive moved closer, watching. The shadows suddenly rippled and bent, and within the shadows, a pale splotch darted out of the undergrowth. Olive froze, staring at the white path. She blinked, rubbed her eyelids with her fingertips, and looked again. Yes—there it was. Something was moving inside the painting, a tiny white shape flitting between the silhouettes of the wiry trees. Olive held perfectly still. She didn't even breathe. The tiny white shape made one more quick plunge toward the path, then dove back into the thorny black forest. And then the painting, too, was perfectly still.

Olive bolted back to her bedroom, jumped into the bed, and yanked the covers over her face. Then she lay as still as she could and listened. The house's creaks and groans were almost covered by the thumps of her own heart. But not quite.

In every place that Olive's family had lived, there had been other people nearby. On the other side of the apartment walls, neighbors moved around in their matching sets of rooms, talking, eating, going about their own lives. Even if Olive couldn't hear them, even if she had rarely spoken to them, she knew they were there. Here, it was just Olive and her parents . . . and whatever it was that flitted through the shadows on that painted forest path.

For a long time, Olive listened. The house moaned and whispered. Wind shushed across the window. Finally, curled in a very tiny ball, with Hershel standing guard on the pillow beside her, Olive fell asleep.

OLIVE WOKE UP rather late the next morning. Her father had already left for his office, but her mother was still in the kitchen, having a third or fourth cup of coffee and arguing with a science program on public television.

"Good morning, sleepyhead," Mrs. Dunwoody chirped as Olive stumbled in and pulled a stool close to the counter. "Do you want toast or cereal this morning?"

"Cereal, please," said Olive, yawning.

Mrs. Dunwoody poured Olive's brightly colored cereal into a bowl and set it on the countertop.

"You remember that I have to go to campus this morning, don't you?"

Olive pretended to remember. She nodded.

"Good. It will only be for a few hours, and I know

you're old enough to take care of yourself, but if you need anything, you can call Mrs. Nivens, who lives next door. Her number is right here by the phone. The only thing you have to do all morning is move the wet laundry from the washer to the dryer. Okay?"

Olive choked on her Sugar-Puffy Kitten Bits.

"In the *basement*? I don't want to go down there by myself!"

"Olive, really. It's just a basement. You can turn all the lights on, and you only have to be down there for a minute."

"But Mom—"

"Olive, if you are old enough to stay home alone, you are old enough to go into the basement alone."

Olive pouted and stirred the sludgy pink milk around in her cereal bowl.

"Good girl. Well, I'm off. Have a good morning, sweetie."

Her mother gave her a coffee-scented kiss on the forehead and fluttered out of the house.

With her mother gone, Olive decided to get the torture over with. After opening the door as wide as it would go, she stood in the basement doorway for a moment, looking down the rickety wooden stairs into the darkness. Then, like somebody jumping into an icy cold swimming pool, she took a deep breath and raced down.

The basement of the old house was made mostly of stone, with some patches of packed dirt poking through, and other patches of crumbling cement trying to hide the dirt. The effect was like an ancient, stale birthday cake frosted by a blindfolded five-year-old.

The basement lights were just bare lightbulbs dangling on chains from the ceiling. Swags of dusty cobwebs hung everywhere: in the corners, between the lightbulbs, over the old pantry shelves built along the walls.

Olive turned on every single light before stuffing the wet laundry into the dryer. She was shoving in the last wet towel when the back of her neck started to prickle. She got this feeling whenever anyone was looking at her, and it had saved her from a lot of spitballs and snowballs. Olive whirled around. No one was there—no one she could see, anyway. Smacking the START button, she tore back toward the stairs, taking them two at a time, even though her legs weren't quite long enough. Back in the safe sunlight of the kitchen, she slammed the basement door and took a deep breath. Then she realized that she had left all of the basement lights on.

Olive knew that wasting electricity was a terrible thing. She had learned all about it in science class. It was almost as bad as wasting water or, worse, throwing a recyclable bottle in the trash. She couldn't leave the basement lights on all day, with the environment already in such bad shape. She would have to go back down to turn them off, and then go back up the stairs in the dark. Olive gulped.

Her parents had warned her not to let her imagination run away with her ever since she was three and had woken them night after night wailing about the sharks hiding under her bed. "Olive, honey," her father had patiently explained, "when a shark is out of the water, it is crushed by the weight of its own body. A shark couldn't survive under your bed." Three-year-old Olive had nodded, and went on to imagine sharks slowly suffocating among the dust bunnies. But eleven-year-old Olive had a bit more faith in her imagination. Somehow, she felt sure that she hadn't been alone in that basement. Someone had been watching her.

With one hand on the wall, she edged down the stairs. The stones under her fingers were rough and cold. Still, having something to touch made her feel a teeny bit safer. She stood for a moment at the bottom of the stairs and looked around. Light from the bulbs brightened a few patches of crisscrossing wooden rafters against the high ceiling. Here and there, it lit up the uneven walls, making patterns in the stone. The dryer chuffed away in the corner. Its hum echoed through the empty space.

Olive yanked the chain of the first lightbulb. Fresh

shadows swooped in around her. She backed up to the second lightbulb. *Click.* More shadows flooded the room, leaving just the glow of the light over the stairs. Olive went up the steps backward this time, determined that whatever was down there in the dark couldn't sneak up behind her. Reaching the top of the staircase, she switched off the final light. There!—something flickered in the corner. Something green and bright. Something that looked like a pair of eyes.

Making a sound halfway between a squeak and a gasp, Olive skidded backward into the kitchen, slammed the basement door, and ran all the way up to her bedroom, where Hershel calmly waited on the pillows.

OLIVE HAD TROUBLE getting to sleep that night. For a while, she thought she *was* sleeping, but then she opened her eyes and saw that the minute column on the digital clock had only gone up by three. Olive sighed. She punched the pillows. She kicked her legs under the bedspread so that it billowed up like a parachute. She listened to the distant sound of her parents talking between the busy clicking of computer keys.

Olive tried counting sheep, but she got lost around forty-two. Olive had never been good at counting. While learning to count to one hundred, she had always skipped the eighties completely. She had gone straight from seventy-nine to ninety while her parents had exchanged aggrieved looks above her head.

"I give up," she said to Hershel, holding him high in the air above her. His black bead eyes caught the dim sheen of streetlights through the windows. "I'm not even going to *try* to fall asleep. I'll just lie here, wide-awake, all night long."

She turned on her side so she could look out of the window. There wasn't much to see. The gauzy curtains stirred in a slight breeze, the branches of the willow tree swayed, and a gigantic orange cat pushed up the window frame and squeezed its body through.

Olive sat up. The cat stood for a moment, sniffing at the air. Then it trotted soundlessly across the room, examining the furniture with careful solemnity.

"Here, kitty, kitty," whispered Olive.

The cat ignored her. It moved away from the dresser toward the vanity, hopping up onto the cushioned chair.

"Here, kitty, kitty, kitty," Olive whispered more loudly.

The cat was now looking into the vanity mirror. Its reflected green eyes glanced at Olive for a split second. "That's not my name," it said. Then the cat looked back at its mirror image and ran one paw delicately over its nose. "Gorgeous," it murmured.

Half of Olive's brain said, *That cat just talked!* The other half of Olive's brain said stubbornly, *No it didn't.* All Olive's mouth said was, "What?"

"I said, 'That's not my name,'" the cat repeated somewhat scornfully.

"But everybody calls a cat that way," said Olive.

"What if I called you *girly*? 'Here, girly, girly, girly.' Rather insulting, isn't it?"

"I'm sorry," said Olive. "I won't do it again."

"Thank you." The cat gave her a slight but gracious nod before turning its attention back to its own reflection.

"What *is* your name?" Olive asked tentatively.

The cat stood up and stretched itself. Its orange fur puffed and settled on its back, and its tail, as thick as a baseball bat, twitched above its head. "My name is Horatio," he said with great dignity. "And you are?"

"Olive Dunwoody. We just moved here."

"Yes, I know." The cat turned his wide orange face toward Olive. Then he leaped down onto the rug.

Olive half expected a cat that size to make a crash like a dropped bowling ball, but he landed with surprising lightness. The cat trotted to the end of Olive's bed and sat, looking up at her. "I suppose you plan to stay for a while."

"Well—yes. My mom and dad said they want to stay here for good. That's why they bought this house. We always lived in apartments before."

"Just because they bought this house doesn't mean that you will stay here forever." The cat's eyes glinted up at her like bits of green cellophane. "A house doesn't belong to someone just because it has been paid for. Houses are much trickier than that."

"What do you mean?"

"I mean, this house belongs to someone else. And that someone may not want you here."

Olive felt a bit miffed. Settling Hershel in her lap, she said, "Well, I don't care. I don't like it here anyway. This house is creepy and weird, and it has too many corners. And . . . it's keeping secrets."

"You've noticed that, have you?" said the cat. "Very good. You're brighter than I gave you credit for."

"Thank you," said Olive uncertainly.

The cat edged a bit closer to the bed. In a whisper, he said, "Keep your eyes open. Be on your guard. There is something that doesn't want you here, and it will do its best to get rid of you."

“Get rid of me?”

“Of all of you. As far as this house is concerned, you are intruders.” Horatio paused. “But don’t get too anxious. There’s very little you can do about it either way.”

The cat turned with a swish of his huge tail and headed toward the window. “I’ll be keeping an eye on you,” he said. “Personally, I like seeing someone new in this place.” Squishing his orange bulk through the window, the cat stepped out onto the balcony and disappeared.

Ripples of goose bumps scuttled from Olive’s toes all the way up to her scalp. She grabbed Hershel’s fuzzy body and squeezed it. “I’m dreaming, aren’t I?” she asked him. Hershel didn’t answer.

In the distance, she heard her father knocking his toothbrush on the sink. The house creaked. A twig of the ash tree tapped softly against her window, again and again, like a small, patient hand.

FOR THE NEXT few days, Olive kept her eyes open. She kept them so wide open that they started to dry out. She even tried not to blink. But three days went by with nothing more unusual than Mr. Dunwoody tripping on the stairs and falling half a flight, and this was because he was reading at the time.

Horatio the cat—whether he was a dream or not—stayed out of sight. Once, Olive thought she saw him looking down at her from an upstairs window while she took a bucket of compost out to the backyard, but she really wasn't sure. If the house was truly trying to get rid of them, it seemed to be taking its time.

Most days, Mr. and Mrs. Dunwoody stayed home, working in the library. Some days, one or both of them would go to campus to use the computers in the math lab or to work in their offices. Either way, Olive had most of the house to herself.

And Olive was used to being on her own. Each time one of her parents took a job at a different college, Olive had to switch to a new school. She had done it three times already. For weeks or months she would be "the new girl"—the one who got lost on her way to the art room, who was wearing the wrong kind of laces in her tennis shoes, who always got picked last for teams. (Of course, if Olive had been able to catch, hit, or kick a ball, this might have been different.) Like Mr. and Mrs. Dunwoody always said, she would get used to things eventually, but it was getting harder and harder. Every time she switched to a new school, Olive tried to be like a chameleon. Silently she would observe the other children and change color until she disappeared into her new environment. But she was getting a bit tired of this. If she were really a chameleon, she would have picked a nice tree and stayed there, wearing her favorite shade of green and never having to turn pink or yellow again.

Fortunately, the start of the school year was still more than two months away, and as far as making friends went, she didn't need to worry. All the people on Linden Street looked just about as old as their houses. There weren't even any young trees in their yards. Not counting flowers, bugs, and a few pairs of socks, Olive guessed that she was the youngest thing on the whole street.

Inside the big stone house, Olive wandered from room to room, staring at the paintings. She had tested every picture frame in the house, pushing and pulling on the paintings of dancing girls and crumbling stone castles and bowls of odd-colored fruit. All of them stuck to the walls as if they had been slathered with superglue. She had even tried to pry the painting of a romantic French couple off of the living room wall with a butter knife. All she achieved was a big gash in the wallpaper. Fortunately, Mr. and Mrs. Dunwoody didn't notice.

She explored the upstairs bedrooms. There were five bedrooms besides the two where Olive and her parents were sleeping. "Guest rooms," Mrs. Dunwoody called them, even though the Dunwoodys never had overnight guests. Olive imagined that all of those rooms were already occupied. Guests were living in each one of them, but had always just gone out whenever Olive went in. It made the house seem friendlier.

The first room, at the front of the house, was papered with pink roses on a pinker background. It smelled like mothballs and very old potpourri. There was a dusty wardrobe in the corner that still had a nightgown and slippers in it. There was also a great big painting of an old town somewhere in Italy or Greece, with crumbling pillars and half-formed walls, and a huge stone archway in the foreground, decorated with stern-faced soldiers three or four times the size of a human being.

The other buildings showed their age, but that arch looked as solid and untouched as it must have looked when it was first carved. Olive peered down the arch's shady tunnel. Beyond the far end, small white buildings crumbled away into the narrowing distance.

The second room was dark blue and somber, with an old hat rack and a dresser full of handkerchiefs, shoehorns, and other useless stuff. The blue room had a painting of a ballroom where an orchestra played while couples in old-fashioned evening clothes danced. Everyone looked very serious and graceful and didn't seem to be having any fun at all.

The third room was Olive's favorite. With its pale violet paper and tatted lace curtains, it looked delicate and grandmotherly. While the other guest rooms smelled of dust and age, this one smelled as though it had been more recently used. A very faint scent of lilacs and lilies of the valley hung in the air.

The violet room also had the chest of drawers full of old-fashioned trinkets that Olive had discovered just after moving in. Olive liked to try on the gloves and stick the tortoiseshell combs in her shortish, straightish hair. The pair of spectacles was there, too, still lying in their silk-lined case.

A portrait hung over the chest of drawers. It was of a young woman—or of a young woman's head and shoulders, anyway—painted in soft pastel hues. The woman's dark hair was pinned up with combs on the

sides, and she wore little pearl earrings and a long string of pearl beads around her neck. The woman was pretty, Olive thought, like the actresses in the old black-and-white movies they showed Sunday afternoons on public television. Her eyes were big and dark, and she had a tiny mouth that tilted up just a bit at the corners.

One afternoon, when Olive was wearing a pink glove on the left hand, a blue glove on the right hand, three scarves around her neck, and all of the tortoiseshell combs she could find, something funny happened. Olive had taken the spectacles out of their case. They were on a long beaded chain, the kind that librarians wear. Olive put the chain around her neck and balanced the spectacles on her nose. And then the portrait *winked* at her.

Olive took off the spectacles and peered up at the painting. The dark-haired woman still stared off to the left, not moving, wearing her little smile. Olive rubbed her eyes. She put the spectacles back on. The woman in the portrait winked at her again, and this time, her smile got a little wider.

Olive waited, barely breathing. Several minutes went by, but the portrait didn't move. Olive started to think that maybe she had hit her head on the corner above the bathtub too many times. She stuffed the gloves and scarves back in the drawer and hurried out of the bedroom with the spectacles still swinging around her neck.

Once, somebody had given Olive a puzzle book with secret messages hidden in the pages. To find them, she ran a strip of red cellophane over the pictures, and the messages would "magically" appear. The messages said pointless things like, "Why did the banana leave the party? Because he had to split." Eventually Olive had ripped up the puzzle book and used it for papier-mâché. But that strip of red cellophane had given her an idea.

In the hallway, Olive stopped in front of the painting of the forest at night. She squinted down the moonlit path. As always, she got the sensation of something lurking there in the darkness—something powerful, something unfriendly. Then she put on the spectacles and slowly leaned toward the painting, moving closer and closer until her nose was almost touching the canvas.

There. She knew she had seen it before! And there it was again: a tiny white shape flitting in and out of the shadows on the path. Olive watched it run, trip on a root, and stumble. It turned, looking over its shoulder. It had a tiny, frightened face, a long white nightshirt, and a scraped knee. It got up, limping, and tried to hurry away. Olive leaned even closer, keeping her eyes on the scurrying figure. Suddenly she could feel the breeze in the dark forest rushing over her skin and through her hair. The canvas seemed to turn to jelly as her face sank through it—

Olive jerked back from the painting. She rubbed her nose. It felt clean—not at all like she had just pushed it into a bowl of Jell-O. Carefully, the way you touch an animal that might not be friendly, she stretched her fingers toward the painting. Her hand went through the frame almost as easily as if it were an open window. A tickly excitement bubbled through Olive's body.

Tugging off the spectacles, Olive hurried down the stairs and skidded into the library. Mr. Dunwoody was working at his computer. He didn't look up until Olive plunked down on the rug beside him.

"Dad," Olive began, "if you wanted to try something, but you weren't sure it would work, and you didn't know if you should try it, what would you do?"

Her father swiveled slowly around in his desk chair. "Would it be safe to say that we're not really talking about *me* here?"

"Not really."

"Well . . ." Mr. Dunwoody leaned back in the chair. "I would say— Just a minute." Mr. Dunwoody sat up again. "We're not talking about anything that involves electricity, are we?"

"No."

"Chemicals?"

"No."

"Violence toward yourself or others?"

Olive paused. "I don't think so."

"All right then." Mr. Dunwoody leaned back again, looking satisfied. "In that case, I would say: Test your hypothesis."

"Test my hypothesis?"

"Yes. Try a dry run." When Olive looked puzzled, Mr. Dunwoody went on. "A dry run is a testing procedure in which the potential effects of failure are deliberately mitigated."

Olive blinked. "What?"

"It means," said her father, more slowly, "try it in a way that won't hurt anybody if it doesn't work."

"Oh." Olive got up. "Thank you."

"Any time," said Mr. Dunwoody, already turning back to the computer screen.

Olive tromped back up the stairs, repeating the words "*Test your hypothesis. Test your hypothesis. Test your hypothesis*" in a marching rhythm.

Hershel was lying on the pillows where she had left him. Olive tucked the bear under her elbow and went to her closet, where she yanked the polka-dot laces out of her sneakers. Then she knotted the laces together and tied them snugly—but not too tight—around Hershel's upper arm.

"All right, Hershel," Olive whispered when they

stood in front of the forest painting. Hershel was poised for takeoff in Olive's hands, his shoelace anchor wrapped between her fingers. "Time to test the hypothesis."

Olive tossed Hershel at the painting. He hit the canvas with a muffled thud and bounced off onto the hallway carpet.

Olive regarded him for a moment, then scooped him up. "Sorry, Hershel. I forgot about the spectacles." She settled the spectacles on her nose and rearranged Hershel for launching. "Now beginning our second trial: in three . . . two . . . one . . . Lift-off!"

This time, Hershel flew through the frame. Olive kept a tight grip on the shoelace. She squinted into the dark forest, but she couldn't see Hershel anywhere in the picture—he must have fallen out of sight, below the edge of the frame. The leafless trees swayed in the distance, almost like reaching hands.

Olive started to feel a bit nervous. Last year at school, the whole class had signed petitions to stop animal testing. She wasn't sure if experimenting with Hershel counted, but it made her feel guilty either way.

To give her mind something else to do, Olive started to count to a hundred. As usual, she got lost somewhere, and one hundred came up astonishingly fast. She suspected that she had skipped not only the eighties, but the seventies and sixties as well. "Close enough," she whispered to the empty hallway. With a step backward, she yanked the shoelace, and Hershel soared back through the frame like a fish on a hook.

Olive inspected Hershel from head to toe. He seemed calm; there were no cuts or bruises or even any dirt on him anywhere. She gave him an appreciative hug and put him back in his place on her pillows. Then she returned to the hallway, took a deep breath, and put her hands on either side of the painting.

Somewhere far down the path, she saw a tiny white shape dart and flicker. Olive leaned forward. Her face sank through the canvas, and then her shoulders, and before she could grab the frame to stop herself, her whole body toppled forward into the dark and chilly forest.

6

OLIVE FROZE. SHE could hear the wind creaking through the bare branches. Patches of moonlight fell onto the white path at her feet. The gravel on the path poked sharply through her favorite stripy blue socks. She looked over her shoulder. Behind her, a frame floated in midair, holding a smallish painting of the upstairs hallway. Olive stuck her hand back through the frame and wiggled it around, just to make sure.

A snapping sound and the rustle of dry leaves came from the thick patch of trees ahead. Looking back once or twice at the glowing square of hallway, Olive set off along the path. At first she went cautiously, but soon her heart settled into an excited beat, like a snare drum in a marching band. Olive almost giggled out loud. It was the kind of giggle someone makes when she is playing hide-and-seek and none of the other kids can find her, even though they've walked past her hiding spot four times. High over Olive's head, black branches rattled. The full moon in its oily navy sky tossed bony shadows over the path.

"Hello?" Olive called. "I know you're here!"

There was a rustle from a cluster of shrubs some distance off the path, to the right.

"I'm not going to hurt you," she promised, moving closer.

The shrubs gave a terrified squeak.

"You can come out," she whispered. "Really."

The shrubs were quiet.

Olive stepped forward and pushed apart their prickly branches. A little white figure inside gave another squeak and rolled itself up into a ball.

"Look!" said Olive. "I'm not anything to be scared of."

"Oh," the ball said, and began to unroll itself.

When it had unrolled completely, Olive saw that it was actually a boy with a large, round face and a very small body hidden in a white nightshirt that was several inches too long. From the top of his round head, pale hair tufted in all different directions. He looked a bit like a tiny, unthreatening scarecrow—the kind that birds end up using as a convenient perch.

"I'm Olive."

"I'm Morton." The scarecrow held out a small, grubby hand. Olive shook it solemnly.

"Are you lost?" she asked.

Morton slowly shook his head. "No . . . He brought me here. And then I couldn't get out."

"Who brought you here?"

"The bad man," Morton whispered.

"What do you mean, *the bad man*?"

Morton squinted up at Olive, his round face catching a beam of moonlight. "Everybody knows the bad man."

"Do you mean the bogeyman?" asked Olive. "Because he's only in your imagination, you know."

Morton shook his head so hard, he almost fell down. "*Everybody* knows him." He looked up at Olive reproachfully.

Olive sighed. "Well, I don't know what you're talking about, so why don't you tell me?"

Morton crossed his arms over his baggy white nightshirt. "I was in my BED . . ." he said very slowly, as if Olive might not understand simple sentences, "and then I HEARD him—"

"The bad man?" Olive interrupted.

Morton glared at her, then nodded. "He was in the garden," Morton continued. "And he was talking. And I got out of my bed, and I went across the grass, and I watched him. He was mixing things, and he was talking to a cat. And the cat TALKED BACK."

Inside Olive's head, two little puzzle pieces went *click.* She held her breath and waited for Morton to continue.

"I made a noise," Morton went on. "The man looked up and he saw me. He said, *Come here, boy. I have something special to show you.* He said I could help him. He said I would be the very first one."

"The very first what?" whispered Olive.

Morton shrugged. "I don't remember. I didn't want to go with him. But my feet went anyway. We went into his house, and then . . ." Morton shook his head, like somebody shaking a Magic 8-Ball to make the next words appear. "Then . . . we both went into the forest, I think. And then the man said, *Good-bye, boy. Don't wait for them to find you.* And then he left." Morton looked down at the hem of his nightshirt. "And then I was by myself."

A cold feeling rippled up Olive's back and across her scalp. "Let's get out of here," she said, glancing over her shoulder. "Right now." She held the branches of the shrubs apart, and Morton crawled through.

They stood up together. In those few minutes, the moon seemed to have moved. Thicker shadows filled the forest, leaving the ground and the path submerged in a deep pool of black.

Olive looked around. "I'm not sure which way to go," she admitted.

Morton, whose head reached the level of Olive's elbow, sidled closer. "I *never* know which way to go," he said.

"Well, all we need to do is find the path," said Olive. "That should lead us out of here."

Olive took a few steps in one direction, with Morton trailing after her like a broken kite. There was no path to be seen. Olive turned and headed in the opposite direction. Nothing. Olive squinted into the growing darkness, looking for a spot that she had passed before—a tree, a stone, anything—but nothing looked familiar.

"That's funny," she said. "I can't remember which way I came."

"He's watching us," Morton whispered. "He won't let us leave."

The back of Olive's neck prickled. She spun around, searching the shadows under the shifting branches. She didn't see anyone, but she felt quite sure that Morton was right. Somebody was watching them. Olive looked down at Morton's round, terrified face. "We'll be okay," she said, hoping her voice sounded surer than she felt. "I promise."

Nearby, a dry twig snapped. In the silence, the sound traveled like a firework. Olive and Morton froze in their steps. There was another sound—the rustle of something moving through the underbrush. Olive crouched, pulling Morton close, keeping her eyes wide open. In the shadows, she saw the glitter of something green.

"Horatio? Is that you?" she whispered.

A furry shape with green eyes emerged from the darkness. It paused, looking at Morton and then at Olive. Finally it gave a long, aggravated sigh, shook its head, and moved quickly to the left.

"Follow the cat!" cried Olive, bounding after Horatio.

But Morton had planted his feet. "That's *the* cat!" he hissed. "The one that talked!"

"I know he talks," said Olive. "I think he's going to show us the way out of here. Now come on!"

Morton shook his head so hard that this time he did fall down.

"Morton! Hurry!" Olive begged, yanking at Morton's hand.

But Morton sat on the ground like an anchor. "No," he said. "I'm not following that cat."

"His name is *Horatio*, and he said he would be keeping an eye on me. He's trying to help us. Get up!"

"I don't have to do everything you say. And you can't make me."

"What?" Olive spluttered.

"*You* have to do what *I* say. Because I'm the boy."

Olive dropped Morton's hand and put her fists on her hips. "How old are you?"

"Nine."

"Well, I'm eleven. So come on."

"I'll be ten in June."

"It *is* June!"

"No it isn't."

"Yes it is!!"

"It's April," said Morton stubbornly.

The last drip of Olive's patience dried up. "Look," she growled, dropping to her knees so that her nose nearly touched Morton's. "I'm going with the cat. You can stay here forever, all by yourself, or you can come with me. *Now.*"

With his mouth squished into a pout, Morton stood up. Olive took his hand. Morton shook her off. This time, Olive grasped his wrist and didn't let go.

Horatio had paused for them, but the moment Olive and Morton were on their feet, he was flying through the underbrush. They scrambled along behind his furry silhouette, hopping over fallen trunks, pushing through bushes. When they reached the pale stones of the path, the cat broke into a run. Morton and Olive hurried behind. They left the thick cover of the forest, and moonlight fell over them, lighting their way. Olive could see the orange hue of Horatio's fur glowing ahead of them. Still running, she turned to glance over her shoulder and had to swallow a scream.

They were being followed. And no matter how fast they ran, Olive didn't see how they could get away.

A shadow, thick and solid as a pool of oil, raced after them from the edge of the forest. It swept up the path, filling the sky. It shut out the moonlight. Olive could feel it turning the air to ice. Goose bumps prickled across her body. A chilly breeze swirled through her hair.

"Hurry!" she shouted to Morton, pulling him along by the arm. With her free hand, she clumsily straightened the spectacles on her face.

Ahead of them, she could see the hanging frame and its picture of the hallway.

"Stay close to me!" Horatio yowled, streaking ahead of them like a furry comet.

Morton pumped his little legs, trying to keep up. Sharp stones jabbed at Olive's feet, but she could

barely feel them. Her heart was thundering. Her lungs ached. Her whole body knew that nothing mattered but getting away from the darkness. And it was coming closer. She could sense it—the thing in the forest, the thing that had been plotting, biding its time, was now just inches away.

Horatio shot through the picture frame like a dart from a blowgun. Olive grabbed Morton beneath the arms and half boosted, half tossed him after the cat. "Hey!" Morton piped indignantly. Then Olive grabbed the sides of the frame and hoisted herself, face-first, onto the hallway carpet just as the shadows swooped in around her.

Horatio didn't waste any time. "This way!" he hissed, streaking down the hall. By the time Olive and Morton had scrambled to their feet, the cat had hopped into the painting outside Olive's bedroom.

Olive turned back and got her first good look at Morton under the hallway's electric lights. What she saw made her freeze in place. Morton's skin, which had seemed nearly white in the moonlight, was actually a very pale peachy color. But it didn't look like ordinary skin. Olive glanced down at her own arm. A normal person's skin was full of tiny details: moles and freckles, fine wrinkles and fuzzy hairs. But Morton's skin was perfectly smooth, and slightly shiny. It wasn't skin at all. It was paint.

She backed uneasily away from Morton toward the painting Horatio had entered. "Here," she whispered, pushing the shakiness out of her voice. "I'll help you through."

Morton took a step backward. "No. I don't want to."

"Morton! Come on, before my parents hear us!"

"I don't want to go in there. I just got out."

Olive wanted to scream, but she knew she shouldn't. Instead, she put both hands in her hair and pulled. "You don't belong out here, Morton," she said as quietly as she could manage. "You're a *painting*. I don't know what will happen if my parents see you, but it won't be good. Now, come on!"

Morton took another slow, sneaky step backward. Then he pivoted on his heel and took off toward Mr. and Mrs. Dunwoody's bedroom.

Olive darted after him. Morton raced around the hallway corner and through the bedroom door, with Olive skidding behind. He scurried around the side of the Dunwoodys' king-size bed and stopped, facing Olive, with the bed as a barricade between them. "Boys are faster than girls," he said.

Olive stared at him, incredulous. Then she leaped onto the middle of her parents' high, puffy bed and glared down at him.

"Morton, stop it," she commanded.

"Morton, stop it," Morton echoed.

"I don't sound like that!"

"I don't sound like th—"

Olive grabbed at him. Morton dodged to the left. Olive mirrored him, her feet sinking deep into the mattress. Morton dodged to the right. Olive bounced after him.

"Can't catch me!" Morton sang. Then, using a bed-post for leverage, he launched himself back toward the hall.

Olive leaped off the bed. In one bound, she was through the door. In another, she was down the hall-way. In a final bound, she was planting her foot directly in Morton's path, and Morton was sliding along the hallway carpet on his stomach, just like a puck on an air hockey table.

Olive threw herself down on top of Morton, clamping one hand over his mouth. Her fingers nearly slipped off of his smooth skin. "Shhh!" she hissed.

For a moment, they both listened. But the big stone house was quiet. Her parents hadn't heard.

Keeping one hand over Morton's mouth, Olive yanked him to his feet and dragged him toward the painting outside her bedroom door. After straighten-ing the spectacles on her nose, Olive locked her hands under Morton's spindly arms and hoisted him toward the painting.

"Hey! Don't push me!" Morton complained, but Olive was already stuffing him through the picture frame like a wet quilt into a dryer. She pulled herself in after him and landed with an almost graceful somersault in the soft field. Morton was sprawled, face-first, on the grass beside her.

It was cool in this painting, but not as chilly as it was in the forest. The air was very still. The sky hung above them like a pale gray canopy, moonless and starless, without a trace of sunset.

Horatio was pacing impatiently on the grass. "If you two could manage to stop wasting time," he scolded, "everything would already have been taken care of. Now get up and follow me."

Olive and Morton got up and brushed themselves off, each trying very hard not to look at the other.

"That is *not* a good cat," Morton grumbled.

"Well, I trust him more than I trust you," snapped Olive. "*You* certainly haven't had any good suggestions."

Morton tossed his tufty head and stomped off after Horatio.

The cat guided them across the field toward the row of houses, his giant orange tail twitching like a banner. The grass under Olive's feet felt soft and dewy. Threads of mist lay across the field, floating in the motionless air.

Gradually, Morton's stomping turned to shuffling. He gazed around, nearly tripping on the hem of his nightshirt. "I think I know this place," he said slowly. "I think I was here once."

In single file, they reached the edge of the field. Horatio led Olive and Morton along the row of houses. In the painting, they had looked small and simple, but up close, Olive saw that they were grand old houses, covered with gingerbread trim and sturdy pillars and leaded windows of every shape and size. The row of houses lined a wide, empty street. No one sat on the porches. No one played on the lawns. No one lit a lamp in the windows. And yet, Olive thought she caught a glimpse of faces staring out at them through slats in the shutters, or peeping at them between closed curtains. Whenever she turned to check, though, the faces were gone.

"I *do* know this place," Morton whispered.

And somehow, Olive had the sense that she knew this place too. It was familiar, but strange, like something from a dream.

"Horatio," Olive asked, "where are we?"

The cat gave a slight shrug. "We're here," he said, without looking back. "Elsewhere."

Horatio stopped abruptly in front of a three-story wooden house. In the dim light, the house looked gray, but by day it might have been any color. Around the house stood a low wooden fence with a gate that was shut in an unfriendly way. The house was silent, and clearly empty. Its windows stared at them like vacant mirrors.

"Why are we stopping here?" Olive asked.

"This is my house," said Morton softly.

Horatio watched them both, saying nothing.

Olive looked at the house again. She *had* seen this house before. She had seen it many times. It was Mrs. Nivens's house.

Olive spun around, examining the street. Yes—there was Mrs. Dewey's house, one door down, with its wide front porch. And across the street was the brick house with the dormer windows. The big oak tree in its front yard was just a scrawny sapling. There were other houses that looked familiar, just with different colors and different details, and there were houses that she didn't recognize at all.

Olive's eyes came to rest on the plot next to Mrs. Nivens's house. Where the old stone house—her house—should have been, there was only an empty swath of land. This was Linden Street, but it was the Linden Street of a long, long time ago, or the Linden Street of a time that never really existed.

"Horatio," Olive began, staring at the unoccupied plot, "where's our house? Why isn't it here?"

"It wasn't necessary," said Horatio brusquely. "Olive,

we must be on our way." He turned back toward the street.

Morton grasped Olive's arm. His hand made a warm spot on her mist-chilled skin. "You're not just going to leave me here, are you?"

Olive looked down into Morton's moony, frightened face, and the irritated voice in her brain, the one that kept saying *GIRLS are smarter than BOYS*, felt a little less sore.

She looked at Horatio for help.

The cat cocked his head matter-of-factly. "It's the closest to home he's going to get."

Olive looked back down at Morton. "I'll come back and see you soon." She paused. "If you want me to, I mean."

Morton took a step back, the frightened look on his face wrestling with a frown. The frown won. "I don't care," he said with a shrug.

"Fine," Olive retorted. "Then . . . good-bye."

"Bye," said Morton, looking away.

Olive let out an angry sigh and turned to hurry after Horatio, who was already moving briskly along the row of houses. Halfway down the street, she glanced back over her shoulder. In the dim gray light, she could see Morton still standing in front of his big empty house, his baggy white nightshirt a pale blotch on the deserted street.

Silently, Olive followed Horatio back across the field to the picture frame.

"So, you've figured out a few more things, have you?" said the cat at last, in the kind of tone that said that this wasn't really a question.

"I guess so."

"I would be more careful if I were you. Don't let anyone know how much you know."

"What do you mean?"

Horatio paused and gave Olive a hard look. "I worded that poorly. Don't let anyone know how *little* you know. Now, what you need to do is to stay out of trouble. Perhaps you should find a nice quiet hobby—one that won't get anyone killed. Like stamp collecting. That's seldom fatal." Horatio turned away and flounced toward the frame. "Now hurry up. We can't stay here for long."

"Wait—stop!" begged Olive. "What do you mean, *get anyone killed?*"

With a put-upon huff, Horatio plopped on the grass and began to groom his paws. "First, the spectacles. You found them. You used them. You know what they do."

"Well, not exactly . . ."

"Can you normally climb into paintings?" Horatio snapped, mid-lick. "You must be wearing them to get in or to get out. In other words, don't lose them while you're inside, or you'll be trapped. Then your only hope is to be released by a guide. Namely, me. And don't stay in any of the paintings for too long, or you'll never get out at all. Not really."

"But why don't *you* need the spectacles?"

Horatio hesitated. He gave his back leg some careful attention. "Haven't you ever heard that cats can see things that others cannot?" he answered at last through a mouthful of his own brilliant orange fur.

"No," said Olive, but Horatio was too absorbed in tail maintenance at this point to notice.

"My coat is simply filthy," he muttered.

"I think you look beautiful," Olive said.

"Do you?" For a moment, Horatio stopped licking. A tiny, bashful look of pleasure flitted over his face. Horatio shook the look away. "In any case, you're not making yourself very popular with a certain someone who is watching you. And what you just did . . . it was dangerous."

"Well, I didn't know what would happen when I went into the painting!" cried Olive. "But when I did, I knew I couldn't just leave Morton there."

"I didn't say you shouldn't have done it. I just said it was dangerous." Horatio got to his feet, looking up at Olive. "You are showing that you won't be a pushover. You might even put up a fight. You won't just let him have his way."

"Him who?"

Horatio turned away, trotting the last steps to the picture frame. "You'll see," he said. Then he hopped through the frame. Olive clambered after him.

Back in the comforting gold light of the hallway, Olive looked at the painting of Linden Street. As she watched, one tiny light flickered to life in a distant window, and she knew that Morton was there, waiting.

WHY DON'T YOU bring this to the table, Olive?" said Mrs. Dunwoody over the last of the dinner preparations as she passed Olive a lighted candle for the centerpiece.

"I've always thought Olive could light up a room," joked Mr. Dunwoody, making Olive's face turn the color of her pink kitten cereal.

Mrs. Dunwoody bustled to the table, kissed Olive and Mr. Dunwoody on the tops of their heads, and settled down in her chair. They all spread their napkins across their laps. Olive dropped hers on the floor.

"When did Olive start wearing glasses?" asked Mr. Dunwoody over a forkful of meatloaf.

"Olive doesn't wear glasses. Do you, Olive?" Mrs. Dunwoody squinted at Olive doubtfully, and then looked even more doubtfully at the spectacles hanging from a chain around Olive's neck.

"I just found these upstairs," said Olive. "In an old chest of drawers."

"Ah," said Mr. Dunwoody. "Was that the experiment you asked me about? You wanted to try wearing them?"

"Yes," said Olive. "That was it. Exactly."

"Well, just don't keep them on for too long," said Mr. Dunwoody. "You could end up having to wear something like these." He tapped one lens of his own thick glasses with the edge of his butter knife. The lens made a loud *clunk*.

"Would you like any lima beans, dear?" asked Mrs. Dunwoody, holding up the serving dish to her husband.

"Yes, forty-six of them, please."

Mrs. Dunwoody scooped a large spoonful onto Mr. Dunwoody's plate. "Forty-six lima beans. How many for you, Olive?"

"I don't know. A small helping."

"Twenty-four for you, then." Mrs. Dunwoody put down the beans and sat back in her chair. "You kept yourself busy all afternoon, Olive. I didn't see you anywhere."

Olive swallowed a mouthful of beans whole. "I was just exploring. Upstairs."

"That sounds like fun," said her mother. "Did you discover anything interesting?"

Olive shrugged. "A few things."

The next morning, both Mr. and Mrs. Dunwoody went to campus for a meeting. Olive stood in the quiet of the upstairs hallway, staring first at the painting of the dark forest, and then at the painting of Linden Street. From the outside, in daylight, the paintings seemed much less menacing. They were stuck to the wall, after all—they couldn't tiptoe into her bedroom while she was sleeping, or tap her on the shoulder when she was all alone in the dark. Then again, Horatio said that they were dangerous. And the shadows streaming after her and Morton hadn't been in her imagination. She was certain of that.

Part of Olive kept hoping Horatio would appear around a doorway, or slide through an open window. She had so much more to ask him. Another part of her wondered if she should climb back into the painting of Linden Street and talk to Morton. Maybe if she asked him the right questions . . . But as soon as she put her hand on the frame, she remembered his angry face, his shrug. His *I don't care.* Olive had heard those words and seen that face before. Year after year, some well-meaning teacher would nudge Olive to join a group of other kids already in the middle of a game. *Can Olive play with you?* the teacher would wheedle, while Olive shuffled and looked down at her toes. The kids would put down their blocks, or their dice, or their dolls, and look up. They would shrug. *I don't care,* one of them would mumble.

Olive's hand slid off the picture frame.

She shuffled down the stairs. Horatio had said someone was watching her. Someone dangerous. Someone who wanted the house. If that someone was the same *bad man* Morton was talking about, what was he going to do? What *could* he do? The only place where anything remotely dangerous had happened to Olive (except for that corner above the bathtub) was inside the painting of the forest. As long as she kept the spectacles safe, and as long as she didn't spend too much time in any one painting, she would be all right. Wasn't that what Horatio had said? Olive ran her fingers down the long chain and settled the antique spectacles on her nose. A little thrill of excitement tickled her stomach. If she was careful, everything would be fine.

So, with the house all to herself, Olive charged freely from room to room wearing the antique spectacles and occasionally bumping into blurry things that might or might not have been furniture.

In the living room, she examined the painting of the man and woman enjoying lunch at a French street café. Through the spectacles, Olive watched the whole scene come to life. Passersby jostled each other. Fat Parisian pigeons hopped. The woman who seemed to be raising her glass in a toast had in fact been frozen in the moment just before she poured her drink into the man's lap. Olive watched the woman flounce away while the man dabbed at his suit with his napkin.

In the upstairs guest bathroom, there was a small watercolor painting of a woman wrapped in a bath towel dipping her big toe delicately into a bathtub. When she noticed Olive watching her, the woman gave an indignant squeal and plunked down in the water, leaving just her head in view.

In the blue bedroom, Olive leaned close to the painting of the fancy ballroom, so close that she could see the swirls and streaks of paint in the dancers' clothes. She wasn't going to climb in, she told herself. She was just going to watch. The painted musicians came to life, clanging and plucking in an out-of-practice fashion at their horns and violins. The dancing couples broke their regal poses and went back to tripping on their hems and stepping on each other's feet. Olive giggled out loud. The dancers glared at her. One tuba player stuck out his tongue.

Olive went back downstairs to the library, where the computer stared at her with its big blank eye. Her parents' work was stacked in carefully planned piles on all of the flat surfaces, and pinned to some of the vertical ones.

There was a painting between two bookshelves that was one of Olive's favorites in the whole house. It showed a group of girls in a flowery meadow, holding hands in a wavy circle. They wore wreaths of wildflowers in their hair and long, soft Grecian dresses. These girls looked cheerful and friendly. They didn't look like they would frown and shrug their shoulders if Olive tried to talk to them. Besides, they were young, and their Grecian dresses didn't look that different from Morton's nightshirt. Maybe they knew something about him.

Putting on her bravest smile, Olive grasped the painting's gilded frame and then leaned forward slowly, until her nose touched the painting. With the same feeling of pressing her face through warm Jell-O, Olive fell through the frame and landed in the soft, sweet-smelling meadow.

The laughing girls stopped laughing. They let go of each other's hands and stood still, glaring at Olive. One of them nervously demolished a daisy; another glanced over her shoulder at the sky.

"What are you doing here?" demanded the girl in the center of the broken circle.

Olive shuffled her feet. She dug her fingernails into her palms. "I . . . I just wondered—I mean, I thought you might know a little boy named Morton."

"Keep your voice down! He'll hear you," hissed a girl with long blond hair.

"You shouldn't be here," said the center girl. "You're going to get us all in trouble. Go away!"

Olive felt several cold, paint-smooth hands pushing her back toward the frame. She toppled clumsily out of the painting, bumping her head on a bookshelf as she landed. The spectacles slipped off her nose and thumped against her chest on their long chain. Olive looked back up at the painting. The dancing girls had gone back to their formation, although now their smiles looked strained and insincere. Olive rubbed her sore head. Morton had been scared of something watching him too, but at least he hadn't pushed her out of a painting.

Olive's footsteps echoed in the dusty library.

She trailed along the hall to the kitchen. Just beside the kitchen door hung a small painting of three men building a wall out of stones. The men wore old-fashioned caps and jackets. They looked a bit dirty, but sociable, like they wouldn't mind having company. Then again, she'd been very wrong about the dancing girls.

Olive hesitated. For a moment, the things she wanted to know wrestled with the things she hated to do. But finally, she put on the spectacles, stood on her toes, and put one arm into the painting, clamping it over the bottom edge of the frame. Then with great effort, she pulled herself sideways onto the patchy ground of the building site.

The three men stopped working and stared at her. Their mouths fell open. One of them dropped the rock he was holding, and had to jump aside before it rolled onto his toes.

Olive swallowed the giant lump in her throat. "Hello," she whispered.

"Well, hello!" said one of the men.

"It's a young lady!" said another man, the way most people would say "It's a flying saucer!"

"Bless my boots!" said the third man. Olive had never heard anybody say "Bless my boots!" aloud before, but it made her smile, and suddenly she felt much less afraid of these three men.

"How on earth did you get in here?" asked the first man, removing his cap and scratching his head. Olive opened her mouth to explain, but the man went on. "Nothing ever changes here," he said doubtfully.

"Sometimes I think I've been laying the same stone over and over," said the second man. "Seems this wall will never get finished."

The first man nodded in agreement. Olive hadn't seen him put his cap back on, but there it was, perched on his head.

The third man was still staring at Olive. "Well, I'll be a monkey's uncle," he whispered.

Olive thought it best to ignore their questions. "What are you building?" she asked instead.

The three men looked at one another. There was a long pause.

"A wall," the second man said at last.

"Yes, a wall." The third man nodded, relieved.

"But a wall of what?" asked Olive.

The three men looked at one another again.

"You know, I can't rightly say," said the first man.

"Weren't we building a house?" asked the third man, frowning so hard that his eyebrows formed one fuzzy caterpillar across his forehead.

"A house. That's it! A house," said the second man.

"There was something funny about the house, though," said the third man slowly. He looked up at the hazy white sky. "What was it?"

"Special stones," muttered the second man to himself. "Crazy demands. That giant cat always in the way. I'd never work for that old geezer again."

"For who? Who do you mean?" asked Olive, her thoughts reeling, but the second man was slowly hoisting the fallen rock back into place.

"Shhh!" the first man hissed at the others, glancing over both his shoulders. "Don't you say that name aloud."

"Something funny," said the third man, still staring straight up into the air. "Something funny about the basement."

"The basement?" said Olive. Something plummeted in her stomach, like an elevator whose cable had snapped. Not the basement. Anywhere but the basement. Olive cleared her throat. "You did say *the basement*, right?" she asked, trying to push the tremor out of her voice.

The three men stared at her, mildly confused. One of them nodded.

"All right, boys, back to work," Olive heard the first man say as she turned back toward the frame.

"Come and see us again, young lady!" shouted the third man with a wave as Olive clambered out of the painting and back into the empty kitchen.

Her heart was pounding. A stone house. A cat.

The basement.

OLIVE RUSHED THROUGH the house, gathering supplies. The more she thought about the basement, the less she wanted to go down there, but the faster she moved, the less time she had to think. It was like jumping into a chilly swimming pool—the moments she spent with her toes curled over the end of the diving board were always worse than the moment when she finally hit the water.

Besides, if she hurried, she might have just enough time to explore the basement before her parents got home and started asking inconvenient questions about what she was doing in her least favorite part of the house. What would Mr. and Mrs. Dunwoody say if they knew that their daughter thought she could talk to a cat and climb in and out of paintings? They would probably yank a strand of her hair and take it in for DNA testing.

In her bedroom, Olive dug through the closet looking for a pair of slippers to wear for protection against the chilly stone floor. But there were no slippers to be found. Olive owned six pairs of slippers, but none of them were ever where they belonged. This was because Olive's body often did things without consulting Olive's brain, which was usually busy with something much more interesting than putting things away in the right place. A second pair of socks would have to do.

Downstairs, Olive rummaged through the kitchen drawers, finding packets of soy sauce, a doll's leg, several used toothbrushes, a few flashlights with batteries that weren't dead yet, and something that looked like a rusty eggbeater but might have come from the inside of a clock. Olive wedged two working flashlights into her pockets.

She paused at the top of the rickety basement steps. A cold, dusty draft blew up through the doorway. Olive tensed and listened. The basement was quiet. She took a deep breath, flicked on the first flashlight, and ventured down, following the beam that sliced a little hole through the dark.

At the bottom of the steps, Olive groped for the chain of a hanging lightbulb. Its weak yellow glow pushed the shadows into a circle. Olive could feel the chill of the damp stone floor even through the double layer of socks. She shivered, held the flashlight up high, and started her search of the basement's twisty corners, where the electric light couldn't reach.

She started with the shelves built into the wall under the stairs. There was nothing there but a few sealed mason jars covered in dust. Olive pulled one down, half expecting to see that it was full of dead frogs or eyeballs in formaldehyde. She found something almost as disgusting: "Pickled beets" said the spidery handwriting on the label. Obviously, it was weird that anyone would like pickled beets, but this probably wasn't the strange thing that the builders had mentioned. Olive sighed, pushing the jar back onto the shelf. She found a few gummy paint cans in a corner, an empty box or two beside the washing machine, and a pack of replacement lightbulbs.

She looked around at the mottled stone walls, at the dust floating softly through the flashlight beam. What on earth had the builders been talking about? What was wrong with this place? Olive ran her free hand up and down her arm, trying to erase the goose bumps. Yes, there was something funny about the basement—not about the way it looked, but about how it *felt.* If the paintings upstairs were hiding something, the basement was hiding something uglier.

There were certainly no paintings down here, and yet, as she sliced her little blade of light across one cobwebby corner, Olive had the sensation, again, of someone watching her.

Olive edged cautiously back toward the stairs, keeping the flashlight raised. Just as her foot reached the bottom step, in the farthest, darkest corner, she caught a familiar glimmer of green.

"Horatio? Is that you?" she whispered.

There was no answer.

Steeling herself, Olive tiptoed into the darkness, following the green glimmer.

"Hello?" she squeaked.

Still no answer.

A feeling of panic pounded its way out from her heart through her whole body. All the tiny hairs on her arms stood up. In her hand, the flashlight quivered. What was in the corner? And how long had it been there, watching, waiting . . . ?

Olive took another teensy step. The pool of gold light from her flashlight washed over the form of a cat. It was black from nose to tail, green-eyed, and sleek. It was gigantic—even bigger than Horatio. In fact, it looked less like a cat and more like a small domestic panther. It sat, sharply erect, with its tail wrapped around its feet. It didn't even blink as Olive approached. Olive was starting to wonder if Ms. McMartin had had

a habit of stuffing her
dead pets, when the cat gave a sharp, soldierly bow.

Olive jumped. Her stifled shriek bounced off the stone walls.

"Good morning, miss," the cat said, and returned to its position.

"G—good morning," stammered Olive, feeling slightly less surprised than someone who had never conversed with a cat before. "I thought—I thought you might be Horatio."

"No," said the huge black cat. "I've never been Horatio."

"I suppose not," said Olive.

"You have her spectacles," said the cat, with its eyes on the chain that hung around Olive's neck.

"Whose spectacles?"

"Hers."

"*Who* hers?"

"Ms. McMartin's."

"Oh," said Olive, touching the spectacles gently. "I wasn't sure whose they were."

"Now they're yours," said the cat.

"I suppose so," said Olive.

The cat regarded her calmly.

"My name is Olive Dunwoody," she said at last. "I live here now."

"Leopold," said the cat. Olive got the feeling that if he had hands, the cat would have saluted. "How do you do?"

"Do you live down here?"

"This is my station, miss," said the cat with another sharp bow.

"Your station? Are you—guarding something?"

"I'm afraid that is classified information," said the cat, puffing out a chest that was clearly covered with imaginary medals.

"I see," said Olive.

She glanced around the empty basement again, wondering what on earth this cat believed himself to be guarding. Then she noticed that he was not sitting on the floor. What the cat was sitting on was made of wood. It was flat and rectangular, and it had a handle made of an iron loop.

"Is that a—" said Olive.

"No," said the cat.

"I mean, is that—"

"No, it isn't."

"Is that a trapdoor?" asked Olive.

"Is what a trapdoor?"

"That. Under you."

The cat glanced down. "No, it's not."

"What's in it?"

"That is not for me to say, miss," said the cat. "Besides, you are safer not knowing."

Olive put her head to one side and considered this for a moment. "What if I want to know anyway?"

The cat blinked. "Look," he said, dropping his military pose. "If I tell you what's in there, then we're in trouble. And I don't mean just you and me. I mean everybody in this house."

Olive crouched down on the floor in front of the cat. "Is there anything I can do to help?"

The cat tilted his head. "There might be, someday. But for now . . ." The cat paused, then said sheepishly, "If you wanted to, you could aid the effort by boosting troop morale . . ."

"I would be happy to," said Olive.

"Oh, good," said the cat. "Then would you scratch between my ears?"

Olive scratched Leopold's glossy black head gamely. The cat began to purr, caught himself, and jerked back into his military position. "Your contribution is appreciated, miss," he said.

From above there came the sound of two car doors slamming.

"My mom and dad are home," said Olive. "I have to go."

"Good day, miss."

"Bye, Leopold."

Olive watched the glimmer of the cat's green eyes grow fainter and fainter as she climbed the stairs. Perhaps the trapdoor was what the builders in the painting had meant about "something funny." But where did the trapdoor go? And if Leopold was guarding it, how would she ever find out? On the top step, Olive switched off the flashlight. The green glimmer disappeared, but Olive knew Leopold was still there, standing guard.

FOR A FEW days, things went on as normal—that is to say, as was normal for the Dunwoody family.

Mr. Dunwoody put the finishing touches on an algorithm he called The Chandelier Conundrum, named after the dusty brass monstrosity that hung over his desk in the library. Mrs. Dunwoody refilled an old prescription for allergy medication, wondering why on earth her cat dander allergies were acting up.

Olive, who would normally have been content painting in a sunny spot in the kitchen, or reading in the library, or digging for buried treasure in the old garden, couldn't sit still long enough to do anything. She was wary of climbing into the paintings, and she had to be extra careful with her parents around anyway. She wondered what was hidden in the basement, but she still had no way to get Leopold away from the trapdoor. She hadn't seen Horatio in days, even though she kept hoping for him to turn up. And, worst of all, she still had no idea what to do about Morton. She was stuck.

So Olive flopped around the house. She flopped on couches, she flopped in easy chairs, she flopped on the porch swing, and she flopped on empty beds. She thought and thought and thought until she could feel the neurons in her brain sizzling out like Fourth of July sparklers. But nothing new came to her. If she was trying to put a puzzle together, Olive realized, she was still missing most of the pieces.

"When you want to do something well, proceed methodically," Mr. Dunwoody always said. That meant: "Take it one step at a time, and don't skip around just because you feel like it." Mr. Dunwoody proceeded methodically whether he was fixing the dishwasher or eating a piece of chocolate cake, and things usually turned out all right. Olive decided to try it.

Methodically, she went to the far end of the upstairs hall and proceeded to search every bedroom. She found one of her missing slippers under the bed in the pink room. There were two buttons, a penny, and a bit of gold string on the closet floor in the blue room. There was an old safety pin in the hall, which she found because it poked her in the foot.

She went back to the violet room and rifled through the drawers, looking at the lacy handkerchiefs and buttoned gloves. But this time, when she reached her arm all the way to the back of the narrow drawer, she touched something that didn't feel at all like a handkerchief or a glove. Olive pulled it into the light. It was a small, worn leather folder, slightly larger than a postcard, with little gold scrolls embossed on the corners.

Olive opened it. Inside, two old black-and-white photographs were stuck to the leather with gold paper tabs. On the left side was a photograph of a youngish couple with round, slightly stupid faces. The woman's eyes looked like they were slowly taking over her forehead. The man was smirking goofily, like he had just seen someone get hit on the head. On the other side of the folder was a portrait of an older man. He had white hair, and a face carved in ridges that looked like they had grown hard with time. He was thin and rigid, with square shoulders, a square jaw, a sharp nose, and long arms; Olive could see them posed stiffly on the photographer's chair. The man wasn't smiling.

Olive had often wondered why people from a long time ago didn't smile for photographs. These days, everybody knows you're supposed to smile, or at least say "cheese." Were people from a hundred years ago all crabby? She had once asked her father about this, but when Mr. Dunwoody started to explain about convex and concave lenses and their properties of reflection, Olive's mind had run away.

It wasn't the man's stern mouth that made him look unfriendly. There was something about his eyes, shadowed by the sharp ledge of his eyebrows. They made him look not just stern, but *menacing*. Olive felt an uncomfortable little twinge shoot down her spine, like a finger running down a row of piano keys. She stuffed the photographs back into the drawer and slammed it.

Olive stared up at the portrait of the dark-haired woman. She looked the same as ever: big-eyed, soft-haired, and pretty, in an understated way. To Olive's relief, she hadn't seemed to notice Olive's silly panic over an antique photograph.

Olive put the spectacles on and looked at the portrait. The dark-haired woman didn't move. Olive took the spectacles off and looked at it some more. She tilted the spectacles so that they went over just one eye. Nothing. She wiped the spectacles on her T-shirt and put them back on. Still nothing happened.

Olive sighed and leaned on the chest of drawers. It didn't make sense. She had first noticed Morton flitting through the forest before she had even found the spectacles. But the rest of the painting hadn't moved—the trees hadn't shifted in the breeze, dry leaves hadn't blown across the path—until she had put on the spectacles. Without the spectacles, the other paintings seemed like ordinary, motionless pictures. And here was a painting that had moved once before but that now refused to move at all, with or without the spectacles. "I don't get it," she mumbled.

"What don't you get?"

Olive looked up at the portrait through the spectacles. The woman in the painting had turned her head and was looking down at Olive with an expression of kind concern.

"Did you just talk?" Olive whispered.

"Yes, I did," said the woman. She gave Olive a sympathetic little smile. "I'm sorry if I'm intruding, but you look so unhappy."

"I'm not really *unhappy*," said Olive slowly. "I'm just trying to figure something out. But I can't tell my parents, because they would think I'm making it all up."

The woman in the portrait nodded. "It's always hard to move to a new place. Why don't you come in here with me, and we'll have a real visit?"

"Really?" said Olive.

"I'd be delighted to have a guest. Climb right up," the woman said, smiling.

Olive clambered onto the chest of drawers and leaned into the portrait's silver frame. She landed with a bounce on a squishy sofa covered with dozens of ornamental pillows, all in different shades of pastels. Long, lacy curtains were draped around the windows, delicate vases full of lilacs and lilies stood on every surface, and elegant collections of seashells and bottles and porcelain rosebuds were scattered everywhere.

In her jeans and sweat socks, Olive felt like she had wandered into the pages of *Little Women* or *Anne of Green Gables,* two books that she liked very much but that she wouldn't have wanted to live in. She could never have kept all those petticoats clean.

The woman from the portrait was seated at a little cloth-covered table, just pouring a cup of tea from a filigreed silver pot.

"Won't you join me?" she asked, gesturing to the other chair.

Olive freed herself from the sofa pillows and made her way to the table.

"Do you take sugar?" asked the woman.

"Yes, please," said Olive.

The woman dropped a lump into Olive's cup and passed it across the table. Olive tried to take the cup gracefully, but her hands weren't cooperating. The delicate saucer slipped out of her fingers, hit the tabletop, and split in two with a brittle *chink*.

Olive shut her eyes and wished that she could disappear. She had wished the same wish many times, and it hadn't come true yet. "I'm sorry," she whispered.

The woman across the table smiled. "Don't worry. Everything stays the same here. Look." She gestured to the broken bits of porcelain. Olive glanced down. The two halves of the saucer had pulled back together, like magnets. Olive picked up the saucer very, very carefully, and turned it over in her hands. There wasn't even a chip in the glaze.

"I'm so glad you came," said the woman, picking up her own teacup. "I haven't had a visitor for ages."

Olive looked around the room while the blush on her cheeks started to cool. "This place seems familiar to me," she said.

"It should," answered the woman. "It's the downstairs parlor of this house."

Suddenly Olive could recognize the shape of the fireplace, the built-in bookcases, the carved wooden panels of the door. The woman seemed funnily familiar too—not just because Olive had looked at her picture so many times, but because she reminded Olive of the kindergarten teachers at her old school. She had the same sweet, slow way of speaking and moving, which always ended up seeming a bit too sweet and slow to be real.

"I grew up in this house, years and years ago." The woman gave a little laugh. "It belonged to my father, and to his father before him. But I'm sure that many things about the place have changed since I was a girl."

"I suppose so. It doesn't look like this anymore."

Olive took a sip of her tea, then plopped four or five more sugar cubes into the cup.

"Why don't you tell me a bit about yourself?" said the woman with a very sweet smile.

Olive cleared her throat and began the recitation. "My name is Olive Dunwoody. I'm eleven. My parents are Alec and Alice Dunwoody. We just moved here a few weeks ago."

"And what do you think of the place?"

"It's kind of . . . strange," said Olive, hoping not to seem impolite.

"Yes, I suppose it is a bit strange. Most old houses have a secret or two." The woman rearranged her string of pearl beads and sipped her tea. "Well, Olive, my name is Annabelle. And you can come to see me any time you like."

"Really?" asked Olive, wondering meanwhile if a person could put more than ten sugar cubes in one cup of tea without seeming insane. "The people in all the other pictures were worried I would get them into trouble. They said there was a man who was watching them."

"Oh, that," said Annabelle, stirring her tea with a dainty spoon. "That is really nothing for you to worry about." She leaned closer to Olive, lowering her voice. "I don't want to sound unkind, but there are some . . . *people* in this house who like to make something out of nothing. They're like cats getting startled by their own tails. You can't believe everything they tell you." Annabelle pressed her cold palm hard against Olive's hand. "Trust me," she said.

Annabelle stood up, brushing imaginary crumbs out of her lap. "I do hope that you'll come and see me again sometime, Olive."

She held out her icy hand, and Olive shook it.

"Be careful as you leave," said Annabelle. "Don't hit your head on the chest of drawers."

"Good-bye. Thanks for the tea," said Olive, climbing onto the couch. Then she smiled back at Annabelle, pulled herself through the picture frame, and hit her head on the chest of drawers.

OLIVE LEFT THE violet room and walked slowly down the hall, past the pictures of the rocky hillside and the bowl of odd fruit, and stopped in front of the painting of Linden Street. The windows of the distant houses were dark. The same starless sky hung above them, stifling the street like a heavy black blanket.

Olive played with a strand of her hair and gazed at the empty street. She tried to imagine living in a painting, like Annabelle or Morton. It would get dull, that was certain. It would be sort of like being sick—lying on the couch, unable to move, while everybody else bustles around you. Olive liked being sick, because it meant she got to stay home from school, and she could read and draw all day. But she supposed that if she were sick for a really long time, she would probably get cranky and impatient. She imagined being stuck like that for years and years, and felt a tiny tug of pity for Morton. Even though he was about as much fun as having a burr caught in your hair.

What if she did go inside the painting of Linden Street? What was the worst thing that could happen? Well, the worst thing would be getting trapped inside and being stuck forever. Olive nibbled nervously on the ends of her hair. Imagine being trapped with Morton for eternity! Still, as long as she kept the spectacles safe and didn't stay too long, she would be fine. Horatio had said so himself.

Horatio. Even the thought of the giant orange cat had begun to make Olive's blood simmer. Giving her little slivers of information, telling her what to do, refusing to answer a simple question, and then disappearing for days! Well, if Horatio wasn't going to help her, she would *have* to find the answers on her own. Besides, Annabelle had said that there was nothing to be afraid of.

Olive dropped the hank of soggy hair. If she were Morton, what would she want? She would want to get out of the painting, of course. And she would want to know that she hadn't been completely forgotten. Olive closed her eyes and tried to picture Morton's round, pale face, but his frowning features and taunting voice kept bumping into the way. Morton might not be happy to see her. But he might be happier if she brought him a present.

Olive dug through her drawers and boxes and closet. There were lots of things she didn't want to give away, especially not to someone like Morton, but there were also lots of things that she could live without: gifts that distant relatives had sent her, or consolation prizes she had won at the school carnival after failing to hit a single balloon with a dart.

With her pockets stuffed, Olive went into the hall and looked carefully in all directions. Her parents were downstairs; she could hear the sound of water in the kitchen sink and the soft voices of a radio news program. Olive put on the spectacles. She grabbed the picture frame and pulled herself into the misty field that rolled up to the painted Linden Street.

Inside the frame, Olive waited for her eyes to adjust. Even the gloomy upstairs hall had been bright compared to the twilight of the painting. Then she took off at a run, moving like scissors through the mist that mended itself behind her.

She spotted Morton from a long way off. He was still dressed in his nightshirt, which seemed a little funny to Olive. Somehow she had expected him to change out of his pajamas. But, of course, nothing else had changed. It was still a cloudy, windless evening on Linden Street, and the faces that peeped through the dark windows at Olive disappeared whenever she turned to look.

Morton had noticed her too. As Olive ran up the street, he froze, his head craned intently in her direction. Then, when he was sure Olive was hurrying toward him, Morton turned his back, raising his shoulders in a long, unwelcoming shrug.

Olive slowed to a walk. If Morton was going to act like he wasn't happy to see her, she would act like she wasn't happy to see him either. She *wasn't* happy to see him. Nope. The little jump she felt in her chest was just relief that he was all right.

By the time Olive shuffled up behind him, Morton was swinging on the gate in front of his house, making it crash as hard as he could. His white nightshirt rippled like a kite's tail behind him.

Blam, went the gate. *Blam*.

"Hello, Morton," Olive said, trying to sound pleasant and nonchalant at the same time. "I came to check on you. Just like I said."

Morton didn't look up. He kicked off the ground with one foot and swung forward so the gate slammed again. *Blam.*

"It's dull here," he said, still not looking at Olive. *Blam.* "Nobody will come outside. Everybody's afraid.

They think he's watching." *Blam.* Morton raised his voice. "But I'm not afraid."

"Yes you are," murmured Olive.

Morton finally looked up. "What?"

"Nothing."

Blam, said the gate.

"I brought you some things," said Olive. "I thought you might like something to play with."

Morton swung back and forth on the gate again and didn't answer. His tufty hair twitched in the air.

"Look." Olive held out the first present. "These are little pellets that turn into sponges if you put them in warm water."

Morton glanced at the packet in Olive's hand. "And then what?"

"I don't know. Then you have sponges."

Morton's head drooped. The gate swung a bit more listlessly. When it shut, it only said *tick.*

Olive tossed the packet of sponge pellets on the ground. "How about this? I brought some crayons and a coloring book. It's Grimm's Fairy Tales. I've only done half of the pictures."

Morton looked up at the book. Then he looked at the fistful of crayons in Olive's hand. "Crayons?" he said slowly. "In all different colors?"

"Yes," said Olive, glad that Morton didn't seem to notice that the crayons were mostly broken ones.

"That's pretty good, I guess," said Morton. He put one foot on the ground, and the gate swayed back and forth.

"And," said Olive, "I brought you this." She put down the crayons and coloring book and pulled a miniature flashlight out of her pocket.

"What is it?"

Olive flicked the flashlight on. A narrow beam of light poked through the dusk and tickled a few of the distant houses.

Morton gasped. He slid off of the gate. Like somebody watching a magic trick, he tiptoed closer to Olive, his mouth hanging open.

"How does it work?" he whispered.

"There's a battery inside it."

"There's batter in it? Like cake batter?"

"No, a battery. It's . . . it's a little thing that makes things work," said Olive, hoping Morton wouldn't ask any follow-up questions. "But it doesn't last forever. So don't turn it on too often."

"Can I hold it?" asked Morton. Olive passed him the flashlight, and Morton twirled around with it, making swirls of gold light against the low-hanging fog.

"Look, I'm a soldier!" he crowed, assuming a stiff position, the beam pointing up from his side like a sword. "Charge!" Head down, flashlight out, Morton barreled toward Olive, who laughed and leaped out of the light.

Morton skidded to a stop. "Now what am I?" He held the flashlight above his head with both hands and turned in place, very slowly.

"An angel on a merry-go-round?"

"Nope. I'm a lighthouse." Morton swung the flashlight in one hand, its glow making a sparkling trail through the mist. "I can write our names. Look." Morton aimed the flashlight toward the low, dark clouds. "M-O-R-T-O-N and O-L-I-V-E," he spelled softly, tracing letters that vanished as quickly as they formed.

"You'd better turn it off. Don't waste the battery."

Morton gave the street a last slow swipe with the flashlight beam, and the soft colors of the houses and lawns flickered at the end of its thin, bright tunnel. Then he let Olive show him how to push the switch. The light disappeared. The street was dark and silent, and somehow emptier than before.

Morton sighed and looked down at the sleeping flashlight. "When can I come out?" he said softly.

"What do you mean?"

"I want to go home."

"But you said this was your house."

"I mean my REAL house. Not in here. The REAL one. I told you, I was in my BED. And I woke up, and he was talking to THAT CAT, and—"

"I know, I know," Olive interrupted. "But Morton,

in the *real* world, this house belongs to somebody else. It's Mrs. Nivens's house. It's not yours."

"Nivens?" said Morton, staring up at Olive.

"Besides, you're not real. You are a *painting*."

Morton's round face folded into a frown. "I am not!"

"Look." Olive grabbed Morton's spindly wrist and flapped his hand through the air. "Paint. Now look at *my* hand. See the difference?"

Morton shook his head stubbornly.

With her fingers still wrapped around Morton's wrist, Olive noticed something else—something that she *didn't* feel. "Morton, you don't have a pulse."

"I do SO have a pulse!" Morton jumped so he could stomp both bare feet at once.

"You're made of paint!" Olive insisted. "Why would you have blood or organs at all? You can't have a pulse if you don't even have a heart."

Morton scowled at Olive. Then he turned his head to one side and craned his neck toward his armpit. He turned to the other side and craned again.

"What are you doing?" asked Olive.

"I'm trying to hear my heart."

"You can't get your ear to your own chest," said Olive. "Here." She dropped to her knees and pressed her ear against Morton's rib cage. And it was funny—there *was* a rib cage there, beneath his baggy white nightshirt, exactly like you would expect a real, live, scrawny boy to have. But there was no sound of breathing. And there was definitely no heartbeat.

"I told you," said Olive. "Nothing."

Morton balled his hands into fists. "I don't believe you."

"Fine. I'll prove it," said Olive. "Let's do some jumping jacks. When you exercise hard, you can feel your heart beating, right? So let's try it."

Olive and Morton spread themselves apart on the dewy grass. "Ready? Go!" said Olive.

They did jumping jacks for a long, long time. Olive counted out loud while the spectacles on their chain bounced against her stomach. Her breath got louder and faster. Soon she felt very warm, even in the cool, damp air of the painting.

"Ninety-one, ninety-two . . ."

"You skipped the eighties," piped Morton.

Olive ignored him.

"One hundred!"

They stopped. Olive flopped down onto the grass. Morton stayed on his feet, staring at her.

"So," Olive panted. "Can you hear your heart? Do you feel it?"

Morton held very still. Then he turned to look up at the sky, where there were no stars, and where the clouds never changed. He didn't answer.

"Do you even feel tired after all of that?" Olive asked. "Do you ever feel thirsty? Or hungry?" She dropped her voice to a whisper. "Morton, do you ever even have to go to the *bathroom*?"

Morton's pale, round face swiveled slowly back to Olive. New thoughts spread across it like a cracked egg. "I think you're lying," he choked. "I used to be hungry. . . ."

He sat down very suddenly on the grass. After a moment, he rolled himself up into a ball. Soft sounds of crying came from somewhere in the ball's middle.

Olive crawled over and put her hand gently on what she thought was Morton's back. He shrugged it away.

And suddenly, she remembered Horatio's warning. How long had she been in the painting? She had no idea. Nothing changed here, so she couldn't gauge how much time had gone by. Maybe it was already too late. Maybe by the time she got back to the frame, it wouldn't let her through. Maybe she wouldn't find the frame at all!

"Morton—I hate to leave right now, but I've got to go. I'm sorry." The white ball snuffled, but it didn't answer. "I'll come back again. And I'll try to find out how to help you. Maybe there's a way."

The ball made a soft snorking sound.

"Bye, Morton," Olive said. Then she ran as fast

as she could down the street, across the misty field, clutching the spectacles tightly in her hand.

There—thank goodness—was the frame, hanging just where she had left it, a square of the hallway glowing inside. Still running, Olive unfolded the spectacles, poked herself in the eye, tried again, and managed to get them on. She threw herself through the frame so hard that if it hadn't been for the sturdy banister along the stairs, she would have fallen over into the downstairs hall.

She lay there on the floor for a while, thinking. Olive was afraid that if she moved, the thoughts that had just gotten strung together in her mind might all fall back apart, like a broken string of beads.

Every time she tried to grasp an idea and turn it over for a closer look, she saw Morton, his round face turned toward that dark, unchanging sky. She remembered the feeling of his warm nightshirt against her face while she had listened for a heartbeat that wasn't there. She clutched at the thought before it could slip away. Warm. His nightshirt was *warm*.

Olive frowned. Annabelle's hands had been cold. They had felt like the porcelain tea set on Annabelle's table, smooth and empty and chilly. They felt like something that had never ever been alive. The girls who pushed Olive through their picture frame had cold hands too. But Morton's hands were warm.

Her mind whirling, Olive stared up at the chandelier above the landing. One of her missing slippers was wedged between its branches.

OLIVE SAT ON her bed, still thinking about Morton. Her reflection sat in the vanity mirror across from her, also thinking. Wondering if reflections worked the same way the paintings did, Olive put on the spectacles and walked into the vanity mirror. All she got was a bumped nose.

She wandered down to the library, where her father was frowning at the computer. "Hello, Olive," he said, glancing up. "Is it dinnertime already?"

"It's three thirty," said Olive.

"Ah." Mr. Dunwoody looked back down at the computer screen. "It's been a long afternoon."

Olive moseyed out onto the porch. The summer day was warm, with moist air making the ferns uncurl happily. The rusty chains on the porch swing creaked in the breeze. She glanced across the yard at Mrs. Nivens's house. It looked very different from the house in the painting. The gate where Morton swung wasn't there. The fence around the yard had disappeared. Instead of tinted gray by evening light, the house was white and gleaming. Neat lace curtains hung in its windows. It was funny, Olive thought. Even though nothing about the house itself had changed, it looked like a different place entirely.

Olive moved through the shade along the side of the house to the backyard, where the thick lilac clumps in the hedges were already turning from purple to brown, and shuffled her feet in the dewy grass. She could hear voices coming through the hedge—women's voices.

Olive peeped through the lilac bushes and into Mrs. Nivens's backyard. It was almost as different from the Dunwoodys' as two yards could be. While the Dunwoodys' was shady and overgrown with tangles of ivy and ferns, Mrs. Nivens's yard had a few carefully tended trees, some tulips growing in strict rows, and grass that looked like it might have been combed and trimmed by hand. A TV commercial would have looked just right in Mrs. Nivens's yard. A dinosaur would have looked just right in the Dunwoodys'.

Mrs. Nivens was sitting with Mrs. Dewey, who lived one house over, beneath the striped umbrella of her little white picnic table. When Olive approached, Mrs. Dewey was talking.

"Well, that's not what Ned Hanniman told me. He's got a perfect view from right across the street, and he said they haven't brought a thing out of that house. It's all still in there."

Olive edged closer, leaning into the lilac bushes.

"I'm sure they just don't know," sighed Mrs. Nivens. "How would they? They don't bother to talk with their neighbors. If I hadn't gone over there and introduced myself, we wouldn't even know their names."

"Sad, isn't it?" Mrs. Dewey shook her head.

"But you know, I personally wouldn't want to live surrounded by all that old stuff. Dusty furniture and paintings and—"

Mrs. Nivens and Mrs. Dewey jumped. Olive had leaned forward just a smidge too far and toppled over into the lilacs.

"Olive?" Mrs. Nivens squinted toward the rustling hedge. "Is that you, dear?"

"Um . . ." said Olive.

"Why don't you come over here and sit with us?" Mrs. Nivens turned back toward Mrs. Dewey. "Lydia, this is Olive Dunwoody, our new neighbor."

Olive, sure that her face was bright pink, squished herself between the bushes and stumbled into the Nivenses' yard.

Mrs. Nivens and Mrs. Dewey both smiled at her sweetly. Mrs. Dewey looked as if she had been made of round parts stacked on top of each other, like a snowman. Mrs. Nivens was thin and blond, and looked like she had been carved out of a stick of butter. Both of them looked like they would melt on a hot day.

"We were just talking about your house," said Mrs. Dewey in a sugary voice.

"Yes." Mrs. Nivens took over. "The McMartins were a very unusual family." Mrs. Nivens said the word *unusual* the way most people said the word *manure.* "I'm sure the inside of the house is just as interesting as the outside." *Interesting* sounded like *manure* too.

"Uh-huh," said Olive. "It's interesting."

"That house used to be quite well-known around here," said Mrs. Dewey. "The man who built it, Aldous McMartin, was a rather famous painter in his time."

"Yes." Mrs. Nivens took over again. "But they say he never sold a single painting. He wouldn't let anyone buy them. That's part of why he became famous—for being so odd. Now and then he'd let people into the house to see the paintings. But for some reason he wouldn't sell a single one."

Somewhere in the back of Olive's mind, a few more puzzle pieces clicked together. If Aldous McMartin wouldn't sell his paintings, it was probably because he knew that they were not ordinary paintings. Maybe he had made them that way himself. Olive's thoughts spiraled like bubbles around a bathtub drain, faster and faster. Was Aldous McMartin the man Morton was talking about? And the girls in the meadow? And the three builders?

Olive was gazing into the distance with her mouth partly open when she realized that Mrs. Nivens and Mrs. Dewey were staring at her with concerned expressions.

Olive started. "I'm sorry. What?"

"I asked," Mrs. Dewey said slowly, "are your parents doing a lot of redecorating? It's such an old-fashioned place, with so many strange things that could be brought up-to-date . . ."

"No," said Olive. "We kind of like it the way it is." And as soon as she said it, she realized that it was true. Their house was much more interesting than any beige two-bedroom apartment. It was more interesting than anyplace Olive had ever been.

Mrs. Nivens and Mrs. Dewey exchanged significant looks.

"Well, I'd better be going." Olive stood up. "Oh, by the way," she said as casually as she could, "did either of you ever know a little boy named Morton who lived around here?"

Mrs. Dewey pursed her lips and frowned slightly. She looked like someone trying to remember the title of a song she hasn't heard in years. But Mrs. Nivens had turned slightly pale—even paler than usual, that is. She sat stiffly, staring at Olive.

"I can't remember anyone with that name, I'm afraid," said Mrs. Dewey.

"No. I don't think so," said Mrs. Nivens. She gave Olive a tight little smile. "Perhaps a very long time ago."

For a moment, Olive could barely breathe. Yes, a very long time ago.

Mrs. Nivens was still staring at her.

"Oh," said Olive, stretching her mouth into what she hoped was a cheery smile. "Thanks anyway." Then she hurried back through the lilac hedge into her own shady yard.

She stumbled into the garden, dazed and dizzy. There was something Mrs. Nivens wasn't telling her. But she and Mrs. Dewey had certainly told her a lot of other things. If Aldous McMartin had done the paintings, maybe he had made them on purpose so that they could be used with the spectacles . . . But Leopold said that the spectacles had belonged to Ms. McMartin. And why would Mr. McMartin have made paintings that people could climb into anyway? Olive twiddled a strand of hair and gazed thoughtfully around the yard.

The backyard garden, a big plot between the crumbling shed and a gigantic oak tree, looked jumbled and overgrown, especially compared to Mrs. Nivens's neat rows of tulips. Olive knelt down in the dirt, but she couldn't tell which plants were weeds and which ones weren't. There were all kinds of strange plants here: plants with purple velvet leaves; plants with tiny red flowers like droplets of blood; plants that looked like open, toothy mouths. She thought she recognized basil and parsley, and something else that looked like mint, but it could just as easily have been a nettle. Tentatively, Olive yanked up one weedy-looking sprout and received a red welt on her thumb.

Sucking on the sore spot, Olive looked around the garden. Could it really have happened the way Morton said? On one night, a long time ago, did he wander out of the house next door and into this yard, perhaps to this very spot . . .

It was a steamy day, but Olive felt a sudden chill trickle down her back. Somebody was watching her.

She looked up. The three stories of the old house stared down at her. Somehow she had never noticed the third story at all. From the front of the old stone house, a person could see only two levels of windows: those on the ground floor, and those upstairs. But here, at the back, something was different. The house's windows were made in all different shapes and sizes. There were large windows and small windows, dormer windows with panes of leaded glass, and windows with colorful beveled borders. Way up high, in a third story, there were tiny round windows that looked like something from an old sailing ship. And in one of those tiny round windows, there were two cats looking down at her.

Olive blinked. The cats sat still, as cats do when they know that they've been spotted. One of them sat mostly in shadow, and the only part of it Olive could see clearly was one bright green eye. The other was large and orange, and very familiar.

Her heart surged. Horatio!

Olive bolted up the steps onto the porch and through the back door. She ran along the hall, grabbed the newel post at the bottom of the stairs to keep from skidding into the parlor, and headed toward the second floor. If there were windows up there, it meant there had to be an attic. And if there was an attic, there had to be a staircase to the attic somewhere, and she was going to find it.

She raced through each upstairs room, searching for the staircase. No luck. She checked the rooms a second time, opening all the closet doors and even looking in drawers and wardrobes, like anyone who has read about Narnia would. She checked every ceiling, making sure there wasn't some sort of trapdoor or ladder that she could pull down. She tried turning newel posts and pushing squares of wood paneling, hoping that there would be some secret lever or button. But there wasn't.

Frustrated and confused, Olive thumped slowly back down the stairs. Whether Horatio was hiding from her, or whether the attic itself was keeping some sort of secret, she was being left out. Olive felt miffed. The miffed feeling grew into a feeling of annoyance, which grew into a feeling that was almost fury. This house was trying to exclude her. But instead of quietly skulking away, as Olive usually did when she was left out, she looked around for something to kick. She gave the wall that ran up the staircase a quick boot, and then felt immediately sorry. It wasn't the wall's fault. But before she had time to make amends, something strange caught her eye.

Halfway down the staircase, just to Olive's right, hung a painting that she had noticed many times. It was an outdoor scene: a small, silver lake under a twilit sky. But this time, as Olive passed the painting, something within it sparkled, catching a beam of light. Olive put on the spectacles. The painted pine trees waved their branches cheerily. The silver water rippled onto the sand. A star or two peeked through the sky. And something small, bright, and gold glittered in the water just beyond the shore. Olive peered at it more closely. Yes, there was absolutely something there.

For a split second, Olive thought about the shadows that had chased her through the forest. She thought about Morton. She thought about Annabelle. And she thought about Horatio. Perhaps Horatio just wanted to scare her. Perhaps he had some reason for wanting to keep her from finding out the truth. Morton hadn't trusted him. Maybe Olive shouldn't either. She wasn't going to let some bossy cat tell her what she could do and where she could go in her own house. With a careful glance around to make sure her parents were nowhere in sight, Olive heaved herself into the picture frame.

Reeds whispered softly around her ankles. Bits of sand slipped through her socks and lodged themselves between her toes. Olive could smell the lake's fishy, warm scent, laced with a whiff of spicy pine.

She walked toward the water. Where the reeds dissolved into a swath of sand, Olive peeled off her socks and rolled up her jeans. The water was the temperature of warm soda pop or cold soup. Olive waded along in the shallow places, hoping to spot the gold thing in the very shallowest water—preferably, right on the sand.

A few feet farther into the lake, something glittered. Olive sighed. The purplish water went over her knees, up to her waist. She tried to grab the gold thing with her toes, but it slipped out of their grip every time. She could feel it, though—something small and cold and hard. She wasn't going to quit until she knew just what it was. Finally, Olive took a big gulp of air, held on to the spectacles with one hand, squinched her eyes shut, and plunged down under the water.

The floor of the lake felt oozy and slick. She touched a few things that were absolutely not alive anymore, and a few things that might still have been, and then she touched something smooth and solid—something that felt like metal.

Olive popped back out of the water like a cork, holding tight to her prize. In the painting's dim evening light, it was hard to see, but the thing in her hand looked like a necklace. It had a long, delicate chain and a smooth gold pendant shaped like an egg. Little swirls and curlicues were etched in the metal. Olive draped the chain around her neck and trudged toward the shore, looking down at the necklace so intently that she didn't notice the fluffy orange cat until she had nearly stepped on him.

Horatio leaped back with a yowl as Olive, and a great deal of lake water, headed onto the sand.

"I'm sorry, Horatio. I didn't see you."

"So I noticed," said the cat. "What have you got there?"

Something in the cat's suspicious green eyes compelled Olive to lie. "Nothing," she said, hurriedly dropping the pendant down the inside of her shirt.

"Nothing. Hmm. Very convincing," said the cat, watching skeptically as Olive struggled to pull her socks over her wet feet. "I'm sure, given a bit more time, you would have come up with something even more stunningly believable."

"I don't know what you're talking about," said Olive.

"Yes, well—that probably *is* true much of the time, but I'm surprised you want to admit it."

Olive crossed her arms and glared down at the cat, whose fur gleamed like bronze in the painting's violet light. "I don't have to tell you everything."

"No, you don't," said the cat. "But it would be a great deal easier if you did."

"Easier? I haven't been able to find you for days! Besides, I know you're keeping secrets from me. Why shouldn't I keep them from you?"

"Because I know what is best."

Olive squeezed a dribble of lake water out of her hair. She was getting a bit chilly in her wet clothes, and more than a bit sick of Horatio's unhelpful answers. "A cat knows what's best for me?"

The big cat narrowed his eyes. "I am doing my best to protect you. And, by the way, you're not doing much to make the job easier."

"It's your job to protect me?"

"You, and the main floors of this house. Leopold, whom you've met, protects the basement. And . . . someone else protects the attic."

"Oh, I see. That makes perfect sense—cats protecting a house."

"If you hadn't noticed," Horatio enunciated, "we're not exactly ordinary cats."

"So just what are you protecting the house *from*? Besides mice, I mean."

"Mice?" huffed Horatio. "It's a bit more serious than *mice*." The cat looked up at Olive intently. "If you must know, it is something much bigger and much stronger than you are prepared to deal with. Believe me."

Something about Horatio's stare made Olive's skin prickle, but she tried not to let him see.

"Fine," she said, breaking his gaze and adjusting the spectacles on her nose. "I found an old necklace. That's all."

The cat gave a sigh that seemed to rise all the way up from the tip of his tail. "Well, you're stuck with it now," he said. "Keep it safe. Don't let anyone see it."

"I'll put it in my jewelry box. It has a lock."

The cat rolled his green eyes. "No. Once you've put it on, you can't take it off."

Olive tried. She pulled and pulled on the chain, but she couldn't seem to lift it over her head. It was as if every time it reached a level with her nose, the pendant suddenly became a magnet—a magnet that was attracted to Olive. The cat watched, with an I-told-you-so expression on his face.

"Keep it under your clothes," Horatio whispered. "Don't let her see it."

"Who?"

"Ms. McMartin!" Horatio hissed, glancing to the left and right anxiously.

"But Ms. McMartin is dead," said Olive, feeling very slow.

"Of course she's dead," said the cat. "But she's still here. Just keep that necklace safe!"

Olive's mind clicked back through all the things she had heard and seen. No one would tell her the whole story. All that she had gathered were baffling fragments of something much bigger and much trickier than she had expected. Still, one fragment kept rising to the top. Olive felt a sudden prickle of excitement and fear—the prickle you feel when your shovel hits something hard, quite deep in the ground, before you have any idea what you've found. "Horatio," said Olive, "what do you know about *Aldous* McMartin?"

The cat froze. His ears flattened against his head and his fur stood up like a fluffy Mohawk. Olive glanced around. The violet sky was darkening, like cloth soaking up a spill of black ink. The air seemed to turn colder, heavier. "We've been noticed," Horatio hissed. "We need to get out of here. Quickly."

In a bound, the cat shot through the frame. Alone in the painting, Olive felt it again: that prickling sensation on the back of her neck, and goose bumps flowing down along her arms. Maybe it was just a cool breeze blowing from across the lake. Or maybe somebody was watching her. What was it that Annabelle had said? That people in this house acted like cats getting startled by their own tails? Well, Olive wasn't going to get scared so easily. She gave the twilit sky above the lake a last, defiant look. Then she pulled herself through the frame and landed with a flop on the carpeted stairs.

"Olive, dear, you're soaking," said Mrs. Dunwoody with mild surprise as she trailed past her down the staircase.

BY THE TIME Olive changed out of her wet clothes, Mr. Dunwoody had dinner ready. Mrs. Dunwoody lit a candle and gave it to Olive to place on the table. Olive helped set their places, poured everyone a glass of water, and even took seconds of the lasagna, but through the whole meal her mind was hopping from clue to clue like a SuperBall.

The paintings. The trapdoor in the basement. The necklace, which hung even now inside her shirt. The attic . . . and the "someone else" who protected it, like Horatio had said. She wasn't going to stop searching until she found a way into the attic and met that someone. Olive got so excited just thinking about this that she dropped her fork on the floor (three times), and knocked over her water (just once, and luckily the glass was almost empty).

After dinner, Mr. and Mrs. Dunwoody suggested that they all play "Forty-two," a more complicated version of Twenty-one that Mr. and Mrs. Dunwoody had invented together back in their college days. Olive knew her only escape would be to say she was too tired and wanted to head to bed, but this would have definitely made her parents suspicious. So she stayed. Her feet jittered impatiently under the table.

At first Mr. and Mrs. Dunwoody let Olive win most of the hands, but by 10:30 Olive lost her entire pile of paper clips and fell asleep in her chair, listening to the sounds of her parents whispering romantically about probabilities and numerical combinations.

She woke up in her bed to the song of a robin and a beam of sunlight pouring in through her bedroom window. After shoveling down a heaping bowl of Sugar-Puffy Kitten Bits, Olive scrambled up to the second floor.

This time, she had a new plan. An attic had to have a staircase or a ladder. And if there was a staircase, that meant there had to be a hollow spot within the walls. If she knocked in the right spot, maybe she would hear it.

Olive started in the upstairs hall. At the front of

the house, she pressed her ear against the wall and tapped with her knuckles. The wall made a low, solid *thump*. She moved her ear a few inches to the left and tapped again. The wall here sounded the same. Olive made her way slowly around the hallway corner, tapping and listening. She was near the painting of the strange bowl of fruit when she heard something else in the wall. It was muffled, and very distant, but Olive recognized the sound. It was the whine of a dog. Olive held her breath. She slid her ear along the wall. The whining sound grew fainter.

On the other side of that wall was the pink room. Olive darted inside, catching the usual stale whiff of potpourri and mothballs. She put her ear to the pink wall, a few feet from the huge painting of the ancient town with its giant stone archway. Nothing—no dog whining, no sound at all. She tapped gently. This time, instead of a solid thump, she heard a light, hollow knock. Her heart gave a happy jump. This painting was certainly large enough to hide a door.

Olive yanked on the huge gold frame. It didn't budge. She wrapped her fingers around its edge and pulled with all her strength. She might as well have been pulling on the wall itself. Olive gave a disappointed huff. Then a new idea floated across her mind.

She put on the spectacles and took a close look at the painting. Nothing changed. The distant trees around the town didn't shake their leaves. The tufts of grass didn't move in a soft summer breeze. Cautiously, Olive put out her hand and pushed her fingertips into the painting, right through the center of the giant stone archway, where the two stone soldiers glared down, unchanging. Her hand went easily through, but she couldn't feel the Mediterranean sun on her skin, or any change in the air. Olive braced herself on one side of the huge frame and pressed her face through the canvas.

At first, all she could see was darkness. She wasn't in the ruins of a Roman village. She wasn't in a painting at all. She was looking through it, just like one of those sneaky mirrors that's actually a window. But there, in the darkness on the other side of the painting, was a thin strip of light. It ran along the bottom edge of an old wooden door. Just above it, a round brass doorknob gave off a reflected glint.

With her heart doing a tap dance against her ribs, Olive stepped through the canvas onto a bare wooden floor, and grasped the handle. The door was heavy. At first it didn't want to budge, but Olive pulled with both arms, and finally, with a low, vibrating creak, it swung toward her. The scent of dusty air, stale and ancient, swept around Olive like invisible snow.

A wooden staircase angled upward from darkness into faint daylight. Olive shut the door behind her and climbed slowly up the narrow stairs. The steps were littered with the papery bodies of dead wasps and bits of brittle sawdust. Olive hoped that there weren't any living wasps to worry about—she wasn't very good with insects.

At the top of the stairs, she stood up, took off the spectacles, and gave the room a long, careful look.

The attic was surprisingly large. Round portal windows cut in each side let in streaks of dusty white sunlight. The ceiling angled sharply up to a point in the middle, with the sides of the room growing lower and lower, so that even a very small person would have had to crouch to reach the corners. But the room itself was not what caught Olive's attention.

The attic was simply heaped with things. There were sewing mannequins and ancient tapestries, locked steamer trunks and glass-fronted cabinets, upholstered sofas draped with white sheets. There were giant gilt-framed mirrors and dusty dressers. There were the remnants of a Victorian washing machine, a small, battered cannon, and something that looked dauntingly like a dentist's chair, or, possibly, a torture device.

And, slightly apart from everything else, stood a tall, paint-spattered easel.

Olive edged toward it. A low stool was positioned in front of the easel, and tubes of paint and bottles of powders were ranged along its tray. To the right, a small table held jars full of brushes, more tubes of pigment, and a palette covered with blobs of dried paint. An oilcloth-draped canvas leaned against the easel's back. Olive reached out, and, with the tips of her fingers, lifted up the cloth and peeped underneath.

The painting on the easel was far from finished. A blue background, which could have been either a wall or the sky, hung behind a wide wooden table that filled the canvas from left to right. On the table lay an open book. And on the book lay a pair of hands. The wrists trailed off into the background, toward a body that had not yet been painted . . . that never *would* be painted, Olive realized.

Her knees wobbling, she put on the spectacles and looked more closely at the painting. In an instant, the hands came to life, clenching the book. Then they moved hesitantly upward, patting at arms and a face that were not there. Olive jumped away, dropping the cloth back over the canvas. Her stomach fizzed and clenched queasily, as if a huge spider had just run over her skin. This was Aldous McMartin's studio. This was where he had worked.

Ducking her head, Olive moved carefully along one

wall, peeking beneath the dusty sheets. Yes, there were more of Aldous McMartin's paintings here, in frames of all different shapes and sizes.

She was about to put on the spectacles again, when a voice from above her hissed, "Oh, ho—a thieving scoundrel, is it? Have at thee!"

Something landed on Olive's back and dug in with four pointy claws.

"Ow!" exclaimed Olive, trying to shake the clinging thing off of her shoulders.

"Yah! Take that, ye scurvy knave!" shouted the thing triumphantly.

"Let go of me!" Olive bellowed, giving the thing a solid thump against a nearby hat rack.

The thing gave a yowl and pulled its claws out of Olive's shirt. She turned just in time to see a furry shape dart up the hat rack and leap into the rafters.

Olive edged slowly around a heap of furniture. Above her, peeping out from behind a crossbeam, was one bright green eye.

"I can see you, you know," she told the green eye. "You might as well come out and talk like a sane person."

A cat edged slowly onto the rafter. It was smallish and short-haired, and covered with splotches of every color in the cat-fur rainbow. Its tail was patched with brown and gold. Its belly and the tips of its toes were

white, except for one hind leg, which was mottled gray and orange. Its nose was crookedly divided into white and black. One eye seemed to be covered in a dark swath of fur, but as the cat moved into the light, Olive saw that the dark fur was, in fact, a leather eye patch.

"I'm Olive," she said to the cat. "I know Horatio, and I've met Leopold, so you can tell me who you are, too."

The cat blinked its uncovered eye at Olive for a moment, as if it were searching for some way around this conversation. Then it gave a little, reluctant sigh. "Harvey," he said.

"And you protect the attic, I suppose?"

"Aye, lass, that I do," said the cat, seeming to regain a bit of his swagger. "Naught that brings danger to this house shall enter it on my watch." The cat gave a leap and grasped a hanging skein of rope, executing a midair somersault that was obviously intended to impress an audience.

"I see," said Olive.

"Sometimes he thinks he's a pirate," said a dry voice. Olive looked down to see Horatio gazing up at Harvey from the floor, and felt her face break into a smile before she could help it. "Other times, he claims to be one of the Three Musketeers."

"The Three Musketeers?" sniffed Harvey, taking a dignified pose on the rafter. "That's ridiculous. I said I was a cousin of the Count of Monte Cristo."

"Horatio," said Olive, casually running her finger along the dusty edge of a mirror. "I was trying to ask you something important the last time I saw you." She glanced up at the cat posing on the rafter. "Maybe Harvey could help with the answer."

Horatio gave a doubtful harrumph.

"I want to know about Aldous McMartin. I know he made the paintings. I want to know *why*. I want to know if Morton ever really knew him. I want to know everything." Olive stared hard into Horatio's unreadable green eyes. "Please tell me the truth."

Horatio looked up at Harvey.

Harvey stroked an imaginary mustache. "Tell the lady," he said.

"Are you mad?" snapped Horatio. "Don't answer me, Harvey. That was a rhetorical question."

A sudden loud whimper came from the far corner. Olive gave a start. "What was that?"

"What was what?" asked Harvey innocently.

"That sound. That whimpering sound."

"I have a guess," said Horatio, with a sharp look up at Harvey.

Olive had already moved to the far corner of the attic and put on the spectacles. Now she was flipping through a stack of canvases. The whimpering sound had gotten a bit louder.

When she came to a painting of a weathered wooden barn surrounded by high yellow grass and a grove of birch trees, Olive heard the whimpering clearly. She *knew* she had heard it before. It sounded like a dog—a dog that was sad, or hurt. Through the small, square panes of the barn's back window, she thought she could see something moving.

"Don't do it," Horatio warned. "Don't go in."

Olive thought of Morton, shivering all alone in the dark forest. "But something is whimpering in there," she argued. She propped the canvas against the wall.

"At least don't bring anything out with you this time!" Horatio shouted, but Olive was already halfway into the picture.

It was late autumn in this painting. There was a nip in the air that brushed the long grass around the old brown barn. Most of the trees in the distance had dropped their leaves, but here and there, one leaf hung, brown or red or gold. The whimpering had gotten louder now, and an edge of excitement entered it as Olive pushed open the creaking barn door.

The barn smelled like very old, empty barns do: like damp wood, and soil, and dust. Something bumped and shuffled in one of the stalls. Olive followed the sound, tiptoeing through the cloudy yellow light.

Inside the last stall, there was a dog. It was a large, dark brown mutt that could have been equal parts bloodhound, spaniel, boxer, and St. Bernard. When it saw Olive's face appear over the edge of the stall door, it gave a delighted yap. And when Olive pulled open the stall door and came inside, its tail thwacked the ground in a frenzy.

The dog was clumsily tied up with a few strings and wires, but it didn't look hungry or thirsty or hurt. Olive supposed that dogs in paintings don't get hungry very quickly anyway. While Olive untangled the knots, the dog licked her face ecstatically.

"Good boy. Down. Down, boy," said Olive. The dog went on licking. "What's your name? Who put you in here?"

The dog didn't answer. Olive felt a bit surprised, but she told herself that she shouldn't be. After all, in most houses, the surprising thing would be if a dog *did* talk, not if it didn't.

Olive was just getting the final knot undone when the dog gave a throaty woof. His whole body, which had been shaking with happiness, became suddenly taut and still. Olive followed his eyes. A multicolored cat wearing an eye patch was seated atop the narrow stall wall.

"So, me old matey," it whispered, "We meet again."

The dog gave a flying leap. Harvey zoomed off like something fired from a musket. "Yah!" Olive heard the cat yell. "That's right, you rump-fed roustabout! Try to get me!" The dog and cat crashed away through the barn. Olive came through the door just in time to see them leap through the frame back into the attic, with the dog's jaws clamped around the cat's long tail.

Harvey caromed off an antique chaise and soared toward the rafters. The dog, who had lost his grip on Harvey, came crashing behind, knocking over the hat rack and managing to shake the cat down from his balancing beam. Olive, crawling back through the frame, watched the cat bolt down the staircase like a flying squirrel, barely touching the floor. The dog was right on his tail.

"Harvey, no! Dog! Stop!" yelled Olive. Nobody listened.

There was a hearty thump as one or both animals hit the attic door and tumbled through the painted arch and into the bedroom. Olive could still hear Harvey laughing like a maniac as the sound of eight galloping paws faded away.

By the time Olive made it to the bottom of the attic stairs, the whole house was in chaos. Mr. and Mrs. Dunwoody had come rushing out of the library, alerted to the crashings coming from the parlor. Mr. Dunwoody was asking questions such as "What on earth was that?" and not getting any answers. Mrs. Dunwoody was sneezing.

Harvey had made a sharp right turn at the bottom of the staircase, leaping from the piano to the mantelpiece. The dog had tried to follow, but had fallen several feet short and landed on the chess table. Horatio had conveniently disappeared.

Olive watched as Harvey catapulted from the hanging lamp through the door to the dining room. "Ha HA!" the cat proclaimed. "No one can capture the wily Captain Flintlock!" The dog answered by knocking over a potted fern.

Harvey and his pursuer skidded down the polished wood of the hallway, Harvey bounding onto a table, the dog jostling the table's legs so that a glass lamp teetered and fell with a crash.

In the knick of time, Olive made a blockade with her body so that both animals were diverted back up the stairs. Two furry blurs barreled toward the pink bedroom. Once more, Olive heard Harvey's taunting

"Ha HA!" Horatio, who had been waiting beside the painting, hopped through the arch and slammed the attic door neatly behind them.

Mr. and Mrs. Dunwoody stood in the hallway, surveying the damage.

"Was that a cat?" asked Mr. Dunwoody.

"That was absolutely a cat," said Mrs. Dunwoody.

"And I believe there was also a dog," said Mr. Dunwoody.

"I believe you're right," said Mrs. Dunwoody.

Olive tried to slink out of sight.

"Olive, dear," Mrs. Dunwoody called, "would you come here a moment, please?"

Mr. Dunwoody picked up a frond of bedraggled fern and turned it over thoughtfully. "We're not saying that you let in the cat and the dog, Olive," he began. "But we hope that you can see why we cannot have animals running through the house like this."

"Yes, I see," said Olive, looking at her feet.

Mrs. Dunwoody sneezed.

"Good." Mr. Dunwoody gave Olive a businesslike nod. "Now, if you make sure both animals are out of the house, we won't have to talk about this again."

Olive turned and shuffled away up the stairs.

For a moment, Mr. and Mrs. Dunwoody looked down at the fragments of the glass lamp scattered across the hall like treacherous confetti.

“How many pieces, dear?” Mr. Dunwoody asked Mrs. Dunwoody with a twinkle in his eyes.

“Three hundred thirteen,” said Mrs. Dunwoody.

Mr. Dunwoody smiled at her lovingly. “You’ve still got it, darling.”

ARE YOU SURE you'll be all right, sweetie?" Mrs. Dunwoody asked Olive for the hundredth time.

"Mom," answered Olive, also for the hundredth time, "I'm eleven and three-quarters. And it's just for one night. I'll be fine."

Olive didn't tell her mother this, but she had plans of her own for that night. First, with the house all to herself, she was going to eat ice cream out of a fancy dish, and flounce around the living room and the parlor, imagining she was a Victorian heiress. Then she was going to find Horatio and *make* him explain about Aldous McMartin. Maybe this would be the key to helping Morton. Finally, when the house began its nightly creaking and moaning, she would bring Hershel downstairs, make a bed for the two of them on the couch, and spend the whole night watching movies, with all the lights on.

"You're absolutely sure you want to stay here?" said Mrs. Dunwoody, tucking a toothbrush and floss into her overnight bag.

"Absolutely. One hundred percent. One hundred and fifty percent sure."

Mrs. Dunwoody gave Olive a conspiratorial smile. "Don't let your father hear you say that."

Olive ran her mother's blue silk scarf through her fingers and tucked it gently into the suitcase. "What do you do at a math convention, anyway?"

Mrs. Dunwoody's eyes took on a glow. "We converse, compare ideas, listen to speeches, go to presentations."

"Is there a pool at your hotel?"

Mrs. Dunwoody paused, looking puzzled. "I'm not sure."

How could anyone not be sure if their hotel had a pool? Olive wondered. Indoor pools were the best part of any hotel—apart from the tiny bars of soap and toothbrushes and mending kits all wrapped in paper on the bathroom counter, like very sanitary presents.

"Anyway," Mrs. Dunwoody resumed, "I've asked Mrs. Nivens to keep an eye on the house tonight, and she'll stop by to check on you. She says you're still welcome to change your mind and sleep at her house."

Olive shook her head violently. If the inside of Mrs. Nivens's house was anything like the outside, Olive didn't belong in it. Olive was destined to break things in houses like Mrs. Nivens's, where everything was spotless and carefully arranged. During just one weekend at her great-aunt Millie's house, Olive had smashed a glass tabletop by dropping an antique marble egg through it *and* had made the toilet overflow. Twice.

"You can call us at the hotel, too, and they will page us no matter where we are."

"I know, Mom."

"My goodness." Mrs. Dunwoody smiled and laid one smooth palm softly against Olive's cheek. "Look at how grown-up you are."

A few minutes later, Olive stood on the front porch and waved as her parents drove down the shady green street. Then she went to the kitchen and fixed herself a gigantic crystal bowl of Triple Ripple ice cream topped with chocolate chips. She glided through the parlor, settled herself regally on the living room sofa, and ate her ice cream in front of the television. It was early afternoon, and at first there were plenty of cartoons to watch, but soon there was nothing to choose from but news and courtroom shows. Olive switched off the television.

The big stone house was quiet. Late-afternoon sun filtered in through the ivy-covered windows, and patches of colored light fell through the stained-glass trim, making soft watercolor hues on the parquet floors. The refrigerator motor kicked in with a tinny growl. Olive got up and stretched. Then she spun around and around, looking up at the patterned tiles on the ceiling, until she got dizzy and had to sit back down.

She touched the spectacles on their long chain. With her parents gone all night, she could go into any painting she wanted to. She could even let Morton out for the night. Of course, it might be difficult to make Morton go back *in* again. Besides, she was no closer to knowing how to help him, and she didn't want to visit him only to abandon him again. And she wasn't even sure that what he told her was true. The only other person—or sort-of person—who would know the truth was Horatio.

"Horatio!" Olive called, glancing around the empty living room. "Horatio!" But no fluffy orange cat appeared.

She went back through the parlor and imagined Annabelle sitting there at her tea table so long ago, posing for her portrait. Olive could almost see her, in her long, gauzy gown, her soft hair piled up around her face. But when Olive blinked, the vision was gone. The parlor was as empty as the living room.

In the kitchen, Olive set her ice cream bowl in the sink. Its heavy clunk echoed through the room. Olive looked around. In their small painting, the three stone masons bent over their wall. Even without the spectacles, their eyes seemed to glitter at her strangely.

Olive wound through the hall and pushed open the creaking doors to the library. Afternoon was already twining into evening, and a few lengthening gold beams glinted on the towering shelves. The computers were off, their screens as blank and dead as the soot-stained mouth of the unused fireplace. "Horatio?" Olive called. No one answered.

Olive trailed up the stairs, turning the lights on as she went. She stopped for a moment beside the painting of the lake, serene beneath its starry sky. Reaching the landing, she turned slowly and looked around, just as she had on her very first visit to this house.

Even though the Dunwoodys had lived there for weeks now, everything in the upstairs hall looked just as it had on that distant afternoon. The ends of the hallway still disappeared into darkness in either direction. Doorways leading to unoccupied bedrooms made shadowy holes along the walls. The frames of the strange paintings—the dark forest, the bowl of weird fruit, the lonely hillside with its distant graves—caught a thin, outlining shimmer of late afternoon light.

The floor gave a creak. "Horatio?" Olive asked hopefully.

There was no answer.

Olive knotted her fingers together. At least her

hands could keep each other company. The stone house was huge, and ancient, and empty. But perhaps it wasn't empty *enough.*

Olive almost ran to the painting of Linden Street. If she couldn't find Horatio, she could at least talk to Morton. Out of habit, she looked around to be sure that her parents weren't nearby. Then she almost laughed at herself. She was alone. That was the whole problem. Olive placed the spectacles on her nose and climbed into the painting's cool mist.

She was getting familiar with this place. It felt almost natural to trot across a foggy field, up a painted street, to a house where somebody you knew lived. This must have been what it felt like to visit a friend. Not that Morton was a friend, exactly. But he was someone to talk to, and he didn't make Olive feel nervous or awkward. And, in a secret, selfish way, Olive was glad that Morton was stuck in one spot. He couldn't leave or change or hide, like Horatio, when she needed him. He was a bit like your favorite page in a book, one that you go back to and read to yourself over and over again, knowing that it will always be the same.

As Olive walked up the deserted pavement of Linden Street, faces peeped out at her from the dark houses and whispers rushed after her, like dry leaves in the wind.

Morton's white nightshirt bobbed and twisted

in the distance. He was in the front yard of the big wooden house. As Olive came closer, she could see him pick up a rock from the walkway and hurl it through the house's front windows. The high, tinkly crash echoed down the empty street.

"Morton!" Olive exclaimed. "What are you doing?"

Morton glanced up at Olive, his face blank. "Smashing things," he said.

"I can see that. But why are you smashing your own windows?"

"I don't know," said Morton with a shrug. "It isn't very much fun to break things that don't stay broken." He scuffed at a bit of grass with his bare toe. The grass unbent and rearranged itself. "Everything you smash here just gets fixed. It goes back to how it was before."

Olive looked up at the house's big downstairs window. The glass had reappeared, as if it had never been broken at all.

"The rock comes back too," said Morton.

And it was true. When Olive looked down, the very same rock had appeared on the path, an inch away from their toes.

"You want to throw it?" Morton offered.

Olive shook her head.

Morton picked up the rock, craned back, and threw it with all the strength in his spindly arm.

SMASHHHH . . . said the window. Olive and Morton watched the fragments of glass shatter, then meld and pull themselves back into the window frame. The window stared back at them, as blank as ever. Olive looked down. The rock was back on the path.

Morton let out a sigh.

Olive cleared her throat, looking down at Morton's slumped shoulders. "I'm sorry I had to leave when you were crying last time."

"I wasn't crying," said Morton.

"Yes you were."

"No. You just imagined it," said Morton, looking away.

"Fine," said Olive. "I'm sorry anyway."

Morton kicked the rock. It bounced along the path, smacked against the porch steps, and rolled back to Morton's foot as though playing fetch with itself. "When do I get to come out?" Morton asked softly.

Olive sighed. "Listen. I've been trying to find out about these paintings. There's a lot I don't understand yet. But maybe, when I do figure it all out, maybe I can—maybe *we* can . . ." Olive trailed off, not knowing how to finish the sentence. She looked up at the empty windows of the big white house. Her house was big and empty, too, but at least she had her parents. She had three cats . . . sometimes. Morton had no one. Only Olive. "Maybe I can help you," she finished, very softly.

Morton snorted.

"What?" demanded Olive.

Morton looked at the ground, speaking into his chest. "You'll never know what to do."

"Well, maybe I would, if anybody would tell me the whole story!" Olive shouted, throwing her hands in the air. "You talked about a 'bad man.' Who was he? What was his name, Morton?"

Morton frowned. "I don't remember."

The fragments in Olive's mind whirled. Mrs. Nivens, Morton, the stone masons, the paintings. And the name that kept turning up, like a book always falling open to the same chapter.

Olive crouched down in front of Morton, who tried not to meet her eyes. "Morton, I need you to remember," she said. "Was his name *Aldous McMartin*?"

Morton's frown got deeper. He started to shake his head, then stopped. His eyes widened. "Old Man McMartin . . ." he whispered.

Olive's heart started to play hopscotch. "That's it, isn't it?" she whispered back. "He lived next door to you. It was him you saw in the garden that night."

A sudden breeze rippled through the foggy air. Olive glanced around. But the sky above them hadn't changed. The same gray light held the painted Linden Street in place, like a specimen trapped in a jar.

Olive reached out and laid her hand on Morton's

shoulder. "I'm going to find out the truth. I promise."

"You?" Morton jerked his shoulder out from under Olive's hand and backed away. "You just took me out of one place and got me stuck in another!" He looked at her reproachfully. "You're no help at all! You're just a stupid girl!" Morton whirled and ran around the corner of his house, out of sight.

Olive put her fists on her hips. "And you're just a bratty little boy!" she yelled after him. "You're not even a boy—you're a *painting*!"

Furious, Olive turned in the opposite direction and stomped away, past the empty lot where her house should have been, past the houses where faces shifted and stared behind the dark windows. Stupid Morton. She would show him.

"Wait!" called a voice.

Olive turned, expecting to see Morton trailing after her, ready to say that he was sorry. Instead, she saw a woman in a lacy nightgown just climbing down from the porch of a house Olive didn't recognize. From other doorways and other windows, heads peered out into the darkness. One by one, a few people ventured tentatively onto their lawns. Olive noticed that all of them were wearing pajamas, just like Morton—funny, old-fashioned nightgowns with puffy sleeves or long flannel suits with nightcaps. In the pale light, in their long, loose clothes, the people

looked ghostly, as if they might fade away into the mist at any moment.

They all stared at Olive. Olive stared back. Her heart gave a frightened little flutter.

"We heard what you said," the woman in lace began. "About *him*."

"You mean Aldous McM—?"

"Shh!" gasped the woman, her eyes widening. The others looked around, watching the sky, rubbing their arms as if they were cold. "He will hear you."

"You're being tricked," called a man in striped pajamas, from a porch across the street. In the dim light, Olive couldn't make out the features of his face.

"What do you mean?" she whispered.

"The cat that brought you here," said the woman. "Those cats, all three of them." She stepped closer to Olive, and the fog stirred softly around her feet. Instinctively, Olive backed away. "Don't you know what they are?"

Olive couldn't answer. She shook her head once.

An old man with a thick beard edged toward the street. "They are witches' familiars," he grumbled. "Imps in animal form, serving evil masters."

"They came to Linden Street with Old Man McMartin," said the man in the stripy pajamas. "They were his servants. His spies."

"He may be listening," whispered the woman in the lacy nightgown, grabbing Olive's hand. "We must talk quickly." The woman's hand was warm, but Olive shuddered anyway. "The cats spied on us. They searched the whole neighborhood. They learned who knew too much, who was suspicious. Then they helped bring us to him."

"I was in my bedroom," said a young woman, from an upstairs window.

"I was asleep in bed," said the old man with the beard. "And then suddenly I was in the big stone house across the street, where I never would have set foot of my own free will."

"I thought I was dreaming," said an old woman's voice in the distance. "But I could feel the night air. I could feel the grass under my feet."

"He said, if we agreed to serve him, he would make us live forever," spoke up the man in the stripy pajamas. "If we refused, he left us here." The old man's face went slack.

"Where no one would find us," said the young woman from the window.

"Where we could never leave," said the old man.

"He wants this house back," whispered the woman, still clinging to Olive's hand. "He needs it. The cats are helping him." She looked at Olive through black irises. "They want to get rid of you."

"Why?" Olive choked out. "Why does he need the house?"

"Go look at the stones," said the old man. "At the bottom."

"Don't trust the cats," hissed the woman in the lacy nightgown, her eyes glittering pools in a face of paint. "Believe us. Go now, while you might still save yourself. Go!"

A sudden wind lashed Olive's face, blowing her hair into her eyes. She could hear the shush of moving air, and the thick rustle of leaves on towering trees. She squinted at the street. Again it was deserted, its porches and windows empty, the houses as lifeless as they had seemed before.

Olive raced back to the picture frame, her feet barely touching the ground. Horatio had said the McMartins' old stone house wasn't *necessary* in this version of Linden Street. Now Olive realized what the cat had meant. This painting was just a place to hold the people Aldous McMartin had captured, like moths in a specimen jar. Olive ran until the painted world around her became like the inside of her mind: a foggy blur streaked with shadows, where things she couldn't see lurked and waited, suddenly rearing into the light when she had already gotten too close.

The upstairs hallway, which had seemed so dark and menacing before, looked brightly lit and comfortingly warm when Olive finally lurched through the frame. She stood staring at the painting of Linden Street for a while, listening to the thundering of her heart, wondering if she really did want to know what the people in the painting were talking about.

She took a deep breath.

Of course she did.

Olive had heard the old saying about curiosity killing the cat. It never quite made sense to her, even when she asked her mother to explain it. "It means that curiosity can lead to danger if we take too many risks," Mrs. Dunwoody had said. "But, of course, if it wasn't for curiosity, we wouldn't take the risks that lead to wonderful discoveries. Roald Amundsen would never have explored the North and South poles. Marie and Pierre Curie wouldn't have done their work with radiation. We would have no penicillin, no polio vaccine . . ." Mrs. Dunwoody had leaped to her feet and begun waving her arms. "Benjamin Franklin would certainly never have flown his kite in a lightning storm! It's *curiosity* that is the mother of invention!"

Olive had to agree with her mother. What could you learn without curiosity, anyway? Only the stuff they made you study in school. She took another deep breath and squared her shoulders. She needed to look at the stones. The stones at the bottom. The stones that the builders must have meant all along.

Moments later, she stood at the top of the basement stairs, armed with one flashlight in her hand and another in her pocket, for backup. She took a last, shaky breath. This was no time to let fear carry her away. The air became colder and denser with each downward step, as if she were wading into a dark, chilly lake. She wasn't going to turn on the lights. She hoped to avoid being noticed by Leopold for as long as she could, and she was sure that he was down there, waiting, his huge black body melding with the shadows.

Olive groped through the darkness, feeling for the basement wall. Her fingertips scraped the stones. She got down on her knees and ran her palms carefully over their surface, following the wall to the corner, then turning, running her hands over the next wall, as high and low as she could reach.

The stones were almost as cold as if they had been kept in a refrigerator, and they were jumbled on top of each other in all different shapes and sizes. She pushed against them, but the walls were solid. There were no cracks, no loose stones to pull out. Olive ran her hand over them in a long, slow arc. *There.* She felt something. A dent in the stone—and then another dent, and another, thin and blunted in places, like something that had been rubbed away. She turned on the flashlight.

In the small white blotch of light, a letter stood out against the gray stone. It was faint, and worn a little bit around the edges, but it was definitely there, and it was definitely real. Olive ran her finger over its carved branches. It was a letter *M*.

Shaking a sticky bit of old cobweb off of her fingers, Olive scanned the stones nearby. To the right, almost in the basement's corner, she spotted what looked like another carving. She had to scrunch down until she was nearly on her stomach to get a good look. This one wasn't a letter. This carving was a shape. Olive rubbed away a streak of dirt, focused the flashlight, and squinted hard. On the mottled gray stone was the outline of a skull. Its empty eyes stared back at Olive.

Her hands shook. A funny feeling, like static electricity, ran down her back and pooled in her stomach. Olive scrambled on her hands and knees along the wall, looking at the stones, and finally wedged herself behind the corner of the washing machine. Yes, there were more carvings in this corner. Jagged loops and swirls that might once have been letters arced above a tiny willow tree, half of its boughs worn away by time. On the intersecting wall, Olive found another letter *M*. This one was attached to a small *c*. The rest of the word was erased completely, but Olive knew what it must have said. Below the *M* and the *c* was a number: 17-something. Olive couldn't make it out. The next digit might have been a 3 or an 8, but she couldn't be sure.

With the flashlight clamped between her jaw and her shoulder, Olive sidled to her left, away from the washer and dryer, toward the largest, emptiest part of the basement. She ran her hands desperately along the wall, brushing away cobwebs and flakes of stale plaster and paint. Halfway along, she found another marking cut into the stone. This one seemed less worn, perhaps because it had been partly covered. Olive scratched away the last bits of dirt and paint. *Here Lies Alfred McMartin*, said the carving. *Memento Mori. 1623.*

Olive stopped breathing. These were gravestones. And if they were gravestones . . . *where were the graves?*

The back of her neck began to prickle. She turned slowly to her left and looked over her shoulder. Two glowing green eyes stared back.

She tilted the flashlight. The outline of a huge black cat, just inches away, glinted in its beam.

"Leopold?" she whispered.

The cat didn't answer.

"Leopold," said Olive as another prickly wave raced up her neck and into her scalp, "how old *is* this house?"

The black outline that was Leopold made a low growling sound. "I can't tell you that, miss."

"Leopold . . ." Olive whispered, not sure that she wanted to ask the next question, ". . . how old are *you*?"

The cat said nothing. His green eyes didn't blink. Olive's words wavered, unanswered, in the cold air.

The warning from Morton's neighbors spilled through Olive's mind like a river of ink, dying everything a new color. She had been fooled. Tricked. Manipulated by three furry demons guarding a house built on gravestones. And here she was, alone with them. For the *whole night*.

Olive thundered up the basement stairs so fast that she fell forward and climbed half the flight on all fours. Between her scrambling feet, she caught a last glimpse of Leopold's glowing eyes, still watching her from the dark corner.

OLIVE SLAMMED THE basement door behind her and skidded along the hallway, whooshing around the banister at the bottom of the staircase. "Annabelle!" she shouted, even though she knew Annabelle probably couldn't hear her. "Annabelle!" Olive pounded up the steps, wishing her legs were long enough to take them two at a time. There were no cats to be seen in the upstairs hall, but Olive turned on every light anyway, telling herself that tonight she wasn't going to worry about wasting electricity. She would leave every light in the whole house burning if she felt like it.

The violet room was dim and silent. A bit of sunlight, fading behind the thick trees, slipped in through the lace curtains. Olive flipped on the lights and managed to put on the spectacles, in spite of her shaking hands.

In the portrait above the dresser, Annabelle stirred with surprise, hurriedly wiping something away from her cheek.

"Annabelle?" panted Olive. "Can I come in? It's kind of an emergency."

"Of course, Olive," said Annabelle. "It's been weeks since I've seen you. I've been hoping you would come."

Before Annabelle finished speaking, Olive had scrambled up onto the dresser and landed on the pillowy couch inside the portrait.

Annabelle sat at the tea table, dabbing at her eyes with a piece of lace that looked much more decorative than absorbent. "Would you care for a cup of tea?" she asked.

"No, thank you," said Olive. "Annabelle, I have to ask you something. But it might sound . . . weird."

Annabelle's eyebrows went up in concern. "You may ask me anything, Olive."

"Well," said Olive, tugging at a purple tassel in the mound of pillows, "you know about this house. So maybe you know about . . . the cats?"

Annabelle tilted her head the tiniest bit. "The cats," she said slowly. "Yes."

"The people in one of the paintings told me that the cats are . . . that the cats"—Olive swallowed hard—"that the cats are *witches' familiars*. That they're evil.

That they're trying to get rid of my family because they want to get the house back for somebody who used to own it. And it has something to do with the basement. Because . . . because there are gravestones in the basement. Really, really old gravestones." Olive clutched the tasseled pillow to her chest like a shield. "And my parents are going to be gone for the whole night, and I don't like Mrs. Nivens, and I don't know anybody else, and I'm scared."

Annabelle closed her eyes. Olive watched her closely, holding her breath. Any second now, Annabelle would open her eyes and look down at Olive with a mix of pity and disappointment, and she would say, "Olive, I'm afraid you've lost your mind. Now, why don't you toddle on down to the closest mental hospital?"

Annabelle opened her eyes. She looked down at Olive. Her eyes weren't full of pity or disappointment. They were circles of honey-colored paint. "Olive," she said, "I'm afraid that what you've heard is true. Those cats are, quite frankly, dangerous. But you can stay with me. You can stay with me just as long as you want to."

Olive felt so relieved, she thought she might cry. "Thank you," she whispered.

Annabelle reached out and patted Olive's hand. Olive tried not to shudder at the chill of Annabelle's skin. "Sometimes it's hard to know whom to trust,"

Annabelle said softly. "And heaven knows we all make mistakes." Here Annabelle made a dainty choking sound and pressed her fingertips to her mouth.

"Annabelle, are you—crying?" Olive asked hesitantly, knowing that many people didn't like to admit it if they were.

Annabelle sighed. "Oh, I've been having a bit of a weep, yes. But I'm just being silly." Then she buried her face very suddenly in her handkerchief.

"What's wrong?" asked Olive, who thought that grown-ups hardly ever cried—except when they dropped things on their toes, of course, like her father had when they tried to haul the oak hutch up the staircase.

"Oh," Annabelle sniffled, "I'm just remembering something. Something my grandfather gave me a long, long time ago, and I lost it. He would be so disappointed in me if he knew."

"Well, where did you last see it?" Olive asked. This was what Mr. and Mrs. Dunwoody asked Olive every time she lost something important. In the single summer when Olive had worn a retainer, she found it in the freezer, in one of her slippers, under the bathroom sink, and in the basket at the bottom of the laundry chute, on four separate occasions.

"It was so long ago," said Annabelle. "I don't know how I could have lost it. It was the loveliest thing I'd ever been given. And—it's funny—but I have the feeling that it is still in this house somewhere."

"What was it?" asked Olive, who was already getting a strange sinking feeling in the bottom of her stomach.

"It was a necklace," said Annabelle. "A beautiful gold necklace with a filigree pendant. Grandfather had it made especially for me."

Olive swallowed hard. She could feel the necklace thunking heavily against her chest, inside her shirt. Somehow, she didn't want to tell Annabelle that she had it. Annabelle might be angry that Olive had put the necklace on in the first place. And Horatio had warned her to keep it hidden—although, of course, she couldn't trust Horatio anymore. Whatever the reason, a little niggling warning in her brain kept stuffing the truth back into its hiding spot. "Maybe if you take a look around, you'll remember the last place you had it."

"Maybe," said Annabelle slowly, "but that would mean getting out of this portrait."

"Can you do that?"

"I can if you let me," said Annabelle, giving Olive a sharp look. "Someone has to let me out. Just like you did with the dog."

"You know about that?" asked Olive.

Annabelle blinked, hesitating for a split second.

Then she said, "I could hear the commotion all the way up here."

"But I didn't want the dog to come out. He was chasing one of the cats."

Annabelle's eyes glowed. "Yes, a cat. But you untied the dog. You set him free." She looked at Olive closely, her eyes like two gold candle flames. "I helped you, and now you can help me. Isn't that what friends do? Will you set me free, Olive?"

Annabelle held out her hand. Olive took it. It was very smooth and pale, and very, very cold.

Annabelle stood up. She smiled. "I haven't left this room in seventy years," she said. She climbed onto the couch and sat, sidesaddle, on the picture frame, still holding Olive's hand. Then she swung her legs gracefully through. Olive hurried after her.

It felt funny, walking through the house with a person who hadn't been there at all—not really—just a few minutes before. Olive glanced up at the young woman next to her, with her carefully combed brown hair and pearls and long gauzy skirts. She felt as though a princess in one of her fairy tale books had climbed out and was waiting to be shown around the house. Except, of course, that Annabelle knew her way around.

At every doorway, at every picture and piece of furniture, Annabelle paused. "It is so good to move around this house again," she said. "I have missed it so much. My house. My old home."

My house, thought Olive, but she didn't say this out loud. It was so good to have company, she didn't want to start an argument.

In front of the painting of the forest path, Annabelle stood looking for so long, smiling and not saying anything, that Olive began to get anxious. Then Annabelle shook her head, as if she was clearing a thought away. "I'm sure we'll find my necklace," she said. "I can tell that it's nearby."

After they had walked all around the upstairs, Olive led Annabelle toward the first floor, but they never made it. Annabelle stopped with a gasp halfway down the stairs.

"There," she whispered. "There—I remember that place. That is where I left it."

Olive looked back. Annabelle was pointing at the painting of the silver lake—to the very spot where Olive had first seen the necklace. Olive could feel her heart starting to pound against her rib cage. Part of her wanted to pull out the necklace, offer it to Annabelle . . . but another part of her said no. It said no very, very loudly. And what had Horatio told her? That she shouldn't show the necklace to *anyone*. Besides, she couldn't take the necklace off. What would Annabelle do if she realized that her precious lost present was stuck around Olive's neck?

"Put on the spectacles, Olive," said Annabelle.

Olive's hands obeyed, even though Olive's head didn't want to. Annabelle took Olive's hand, and again Olive noticed the icy cold of Annabelle's touch. With

Annabelle leading the way, they climbed into the picture of the silvery lake.

Annabelle headed toward the water, her tiny pointed boots making sharp prints in the sand. Olive stumbled behind her. The ripples in the lake seemed to get rougher, wilder, as they approached.

Annabelle stopped at the shore. She glanced up and down the beach, where the lake had scattered small red and black stones, and looked into the water. "I think it is a few feet farther out in the water," she said to Olive without turning. "There is an old rowboat in the reeds over there. Get it."

Olive looked where Annabelle was pointing. To her surprise, there was a weathered wooden rowboat half covered by the waving reeds. She hadn't noticed it before. Olive dragged the boat along in the shallow water until it stood in front of Annabelle. Annabelle climbed in first, taking up the oar, and Olive climbed in after her.

Annabelle began to row. For a delicate-looking woman, she rowed powerfully.

"Do you see anything?" asked Olive, peering out into the water.

"Not yet," said Annabelle.

They were quickly beyond the shallows, but Annabelle kept rowing. Soon they were ten feet, twenty feet, fifty feet from the shore.

"I can't see the bottom anymore," said Olive nervously. "Do you think the necklace is out this far?"

This time Annabelle didn't answer. She rowed farther into center of the lake. Here the water no longer looked silver, but black, and the evening sky above looked cold and distant.

"Would you like me to take a turn rowing?" offered Olive, trying to keep the tremble out of her voice.

"I don't think so," said Annabelle. Then, as Olive watched, Annabelle hurled the wooden oar far out into the water. The waves were choppy now, and the oar bobbed and flickered in the ridges, moving farther and farther away.

"You see, I know where the necklace is," Annabelle said softly, giving Olive the tiniest of smiles. "I knew even before you let me out of my portrait."

"You did?" Olive gulped.

"Yes. I've been watching you. You've been in and out of paintings all over this house. Sometimes you've only gotten in the way—like when you took that little boy back out of the forest. But other times you've done just as we wished, like setting the dog loose. And letting me out." Annabelle leaned closer to Olive. Her voice was low. "And I know something else. I know that you can't take the necklace off now that you've put it on. That's how it works. You will wear it until you die."

"Until you die?" Olive whispered.

"Not me," Annabelle said. "I've already died. *You*."

Annabelle stood up. The boat rocked crazily. The waves plunged and rose. And then Olive saw something she had seen twice before—a thick, black shadow, pouring across the sky like oil, turning everything beneath it cold and dark.

Annabelle raised a hand. Between the rowboat and the shore, a path of smooth black stones appeared on the water. Annabelle stepped out onto the path, making her way gracefully toward the land. The stones dissolved into the water behind her.

She glanced back once at Olive, who was clinging to the side of the boat in the roiling black water. "Good-bye, Olive," she said. "Someone should have told you not to take things that don't belong to you. Speaking of which . . ." Annabelle made a sign in the air. Olive felt a wind as strong as a fist hit her rib cage. It ripped the spectacles from around her neck, carried them through the air, and dropped them into Annabelle's waiting hand. Then Annabelle walked to the end of the path, onto the shore, and into the darkness.

A large wave lifted the rickety little boat. For a second the boat hovered there on the crest of the wave, and Olive had the chance to look around at the shining, splashing darkness. Then the boat plunged back

down the wave's other side, dragging Olive—and, a second later, Olive's stomach—with it.

She hung on to the slippery wood with both hands. "Help!" she yelled to nobody at all. "Help me!"

A flood of cold water splashed over the low sides, leaving Olive drenched. The wind was growing stronger, the waves were getting higher, and Olive was quite sure that she was screaming, even though she couldn't hear her own voice.

Another wave pummeled the boat's side. Olive braced herself against the boat's low walls, trying to balance it with her weight, but when the next huge wave crashed into the boat, Olive was tossed out of it like one noodle slipping out of a spoon and landing back in a huge bowl of soup.

For a few seconds everything was black. Black, and cold, and *wet*. Olive realized that she was beneath the murky water of the lake, but with the darkness solid as marble on every side, she had no idea which way was up. Even with her eyes wide open, she couldn't see a thing. This was probably for the best, Olive decided—she didn't want to know just what else might be swimming beneath her in the black water of the lake.

Her lungs were already starting to ache. Olive made her body go limp, hoping she would float to the surface like a bubble. Sure enough, she felt herself being pulled very slowly in one direction. Olive kicked her legs, paddling wildly, her lungs threatening to burst—and then she was breaking through the surface, taking in huge gulps of air.

The lake was still rocking like an overcrowded trampoline. Olive, struggling to keep her head above the water, was hoisted and dropped by rows of waves. She squinted through the darkness. There—in the distance—she could see a small square of light, where the picture frame held a lamplit view of the stairs.

Olive began to paddle toward it, holding her breath whenever the waves crashed over her head. Once or twice, she swallowed a mouthful of lake water. It was mucky and oily, and tasted like molding leaves. The frigid water was turning her feet numb. She was exhausted; her arms and shoulders ached, but the little square of light was coming closer.

A towering wave smacked her like a swatter landing on a housefly. The force of it pushed her down under the surface, but this time, Olive felt her feet touch the rocks at the bottom of the lake. She gave a strong push with both legs. Soon she was paddling, then crawling, onto the wet sand of the shore.

Olive knelt there for a moment, panting and gasping. Then she took off at a run for the picture frame.

"Somebody!" Olive yelled. "Anybody! Help me!" The shadows in the sky pulsed and thundered above her. Olive could hear the darkness roaring all around;

she could feel it, grasping at her arms and legs, trying to pull her back. Olive glanced down at the shadows sweeping around her body. Was she imagining it, or were her feet changing color? Yes—they looked grayer, and different, somehow. They were streakier. Shinier. They looked like they had been made of paint.

With a rush of nausea, Olive realized what Horatio had meant about being trapped in the painting for too long. He had been telling the truth after all. Was this what had happened to Morton? And to the neighbors? And to the men who had laid the gravestones in the basement? Revelation pummeled Olive like another great black wave. Maybe the cats had been telling the truth the whole time. And maybe it was already too late.

Olive clamped her hands around the silver edges of the frame. "Horatio!" she screamed. "HORATIO!"

"Well, back up if you want me to get in there," a voice snapped.

Olive staggered sideways, and the huge orange cat soared through the frame. Horatio glanced up at Olive through the dark, swirling air, and the irritated expression on his face disappeared for a split second. "Are you all right?" he shouted over the storm.

"Mostly. My feet—" Olive looked down. The shiny streaks of paint had climbed past her ankles. Her toes felt numb.

"Hang on to my tail! Hurry!" Horatio bounded back through the frame.

Olive locked one hand around Horatio's tail and the other around the picture frame, hoisted herself out of the painting, and shot across the hallway stairs with such force that she hit the opposite banister and rolled all the way down the steps onto the rug at the bottom of the staircase.

Olive pulled herself up onto her elbows and examined her legs. Little tickling waves of warmth were zinging down from her knees to the tips of her toes. If she hadn't known better, Olive would have thought her legs had fallen asleep. Her feet looked like they had always looked, like they were made of bones and skin. She wiggled her toes. So far, so good.

Horatio huffed and paced on the step above her. "What did I tell you?" he demanded. "I said, *Don't lose the spectacles*. I said, *If you lose them, you won't be able to get out again*. For more than a century, nobody lost those spectacles. But *you* manage to lose them in just a few weeks and to almost get yourself killed because of it. It's astonishing, really. The *one thing* I've told you to do, the most important thing—"

"But I didn't lose them!" shouted Olive, who had finally gotten her breath back. "She took them."

"She?" Horatio crouched on the step, staring intently at Olive. "She who?"

The doorbell rang.

Horatio bolted up the stairs. Olive clambered to her feet, which still felt a bit numb, and pushed the wet strands of hair out of her eyes. Her saturated sweat socks made small *squish, squish* sounds as she walked along the hall to the door.

Olive peeked through the keyhole. Mrs. Nivens stood on the porch. She wore a spotless apron, a perfectly ironed dress, and a smile that, when Olive opened the door, looked like it might slide off of her face and shatter on the stoop.

"Good evening, Mrs. Nivens," said Olive politely.

"Hello, Olive, dear." Mrs. Nivens looked down at the pool of water that was forming around Olive's feet. "Were you—swimming?"

"I was just taking a shower," said Olive.

"In your clothes?" asked Mrs. Nivens, whose voice had gone up a key.

"They were dirty too," said Olive.

"I see." Mrs. Nivens nodded slowly. A few droplets of water from the pool at Olive's feet trailed over the doorjamb and plopped onto the porch.

"Well, I brought you a plate of chocolate raisin cookies," Mrs. Nivens went on bravely, holding out a foil-wrapped plate. Olive took the plate in her wet hands. "But don't spoil your dinner, now."

"Thank you very much, Mrs. Nivens," said Olive.

"You're welcome," said Mrs. Nivens. She gave Olive a long, hard look. "Are you sure you're all right, Olive?"

Olive nodded hard, hoping Mrs. Nivens would leave before a talking cat or escapee from a painting showed up.

"It's a funny old house, isn't it?" Mrs. Nivens murmured. Her eyes left Olive's face and slowly scanned the hallway, trailing up the stairs. "So much history. I haven't been inside in ages, but I can still remember almost every detail—"

"Uh-huh," said Olive quickly. "Well, I'll call you if I need anything. Thank you again for the cookies." She slammed the door shut before Mrs. Nivens could say another word.

Olive peeked through the front window and watched Mrs. Nivens go side-wise down the porch stairs, keeping one eye on the house, before scuttling down the walk toward her own house. Then Olive locked the door. She didn't want Mrs. Nivens's help. There was something about the way Mrs. Nivens looked at her that made Olive want to tell lies. Olive leaned against the door, keeping her eyes peeled, and absently munched a cookie. If Annabelle was waiting for Olive to drown so that she could get the necklace back, she probably wouldn't have gone far.

Olive wondered how one went about getting rid of

a person who had come out of a painting. Annabelle wasn't alive, after all. What did people use to destroy paint? Soap and water? Turpentine? A paint scraper?

Olive was brushing a streak of crumbs off of her wet clothes when a furry orange cannonball shot down the stairs in two bounds and crashed into Olive's shins.

"Now is the time!" puffed Horatio, staggering onto his feet. "We need your help—Ms. McMartin is loose!"

Olive, Horatio, and Harvey, freshly escaped from the attic, held a hushed conference in one of the upstairs bathtubs. There were no paintings in this bathroom, and Horatio had selected the spot as the safest base of operations.

Still wet and wobbly, Olive huddled against the tub wall and gave both cats a long, cautious look. Could they really be what Morton's neighbors had said? She glanced from one to the other. Harvey's eye patch had disappeared. Instead, he was wearing a small metal breastplate, which looked as if it had been made from tuna cans and pop tabs.

"Who does he think he is tonight?" Olive whispered to Horatio.

"Lancelot du Lac," Horatio whispered back.

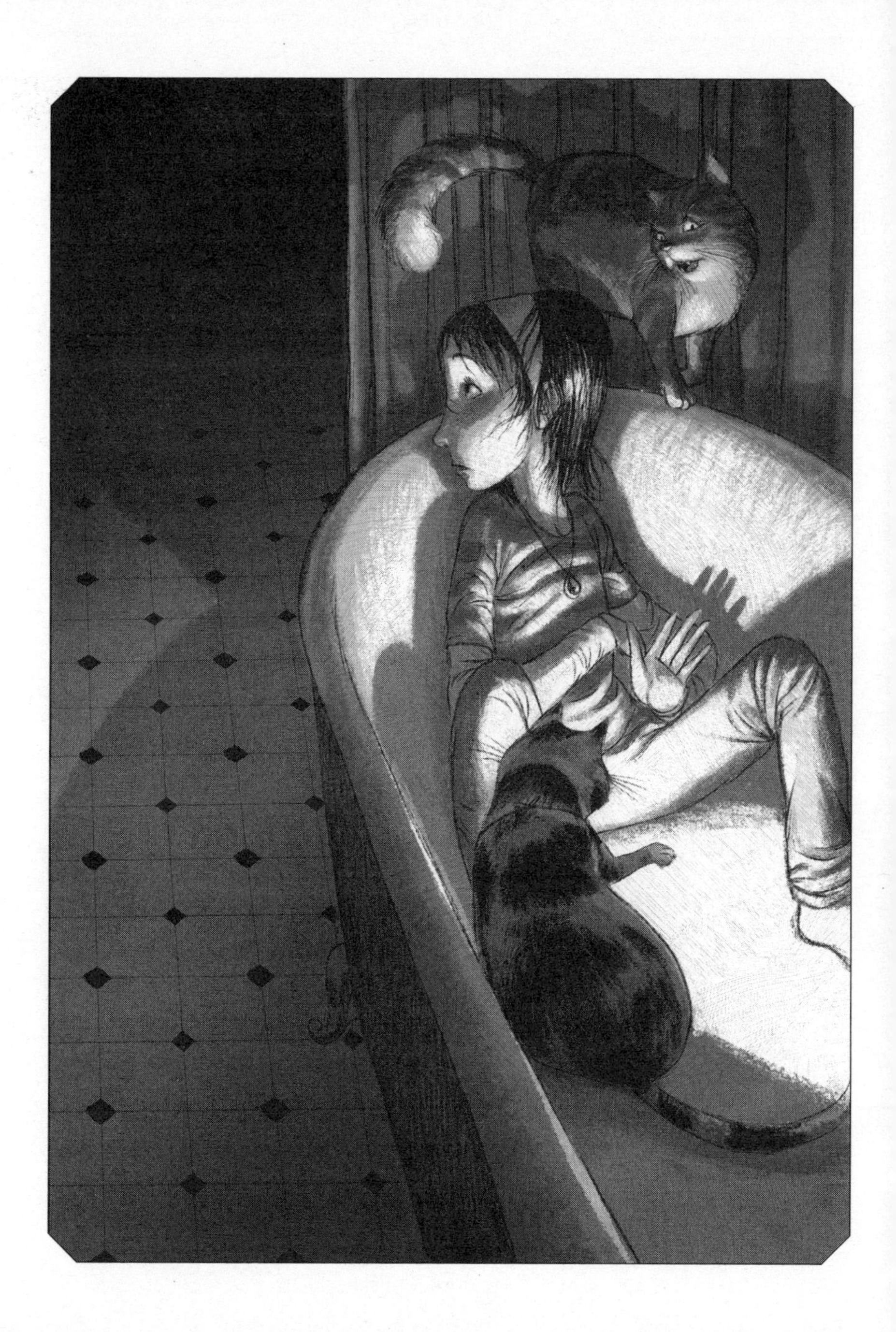

Harvey gave Olive a gallant bow.

"First things first," said Horatio. "Have you still got the necklace?"

Olive reached into the neck of her damp shirt and slowly, shakily, pulled out the pendant. Horatio gave a sigh of relief.

Harvey's eyes went wild.

"Blackpaw's booty!" he exclaimed. "The buried treasure of the pirate king!"

Horatio's eyes became two thin green slits. "It was you?" he hissed. "You knew where it was all along?" His head swiveled toward Harvey like the gun on an army tank. "You took it from Ms. McMartin's body and decided to *play pirate with it?!*"

Thick orange fur bristling, Horatio pulled himself into pre-launch position.

"You dare to challenge zee greatest knight of all?" growled Harvey in a French accent, turning into a smaller but equally bristly hump.

"Wait! Wait!" said Olive, throwing herself between the cats and pinning them to the tub walls. Harvey let out an angry hiss above her elbow. "We can't waste time like this!" she insisted. "I need to know what's going on here. Then we can make a plan. Agreed?"

"Fine," Horatio muttered.

"I grant my opponent's plea for mercy," said Harvey magnanimously.

"Good." Olive took a deep breath and looked closely at both cats. "But first, I need to know one thing." Olive tried to keep her voice from wavering. "Do you actually work for Aldous McMartin? Are you . . . *witches' familiars?*"

Harvey and Horatio glanced across the tub at each other. Harvey looked down at Olive's toes. Finally, Horatio sighed. "We have belonged to the McMartin family for hundreds of years," he said. "Longer than any of us can remember. And, yes, they are a line of powerful witches, and, yes, it was our role to serve them."

"Even if we didn't want to," Harvey put in, still looking at Olive's toes.

"So why wouldn't Leopold just tell me how old he was?" asked Olive.

"Can you remember what you had for dinner last Monday?" Horatio challenged. "Try remembering your age if you predate paper."

Olive tried to imagine this. She couldn't. In fact, she couldn't even remember when paper was invented.

"Aldous McMartin was the worst of the lot," Horatio went on. "Greedy, cruel, dangerous. And brilliant. He was so hated and feared in Scotland that one night a band of townspeople set fire to the McMartin homestead, where the family had lived for centuries. They destroyed the family plot, smashed the headstones, dug up the graves, and burned what they found. After escaping to America, Aldous had everything that remained of the family graveyard brought here—"

"Everything?" squeaked Olive, hugging her knees.

Horatio gave her a sharp look. "—and built a new home for the McMartin line on top of it, to preserve the power of the family." Here Horatio paused, studying his front paw. "But things didn't work out quite as Aldous had hoped."

"What do you mean?" asked Olive.

"His son, Albert, was a huge disappointment."

"'E was nice," Harvey piped up. "Nice and stupeed."

"Albert had no talent for witchcraft. In fact, he had no talents at all. The only good thing Albert ever did, as far as Aldous was concerned, was have a daughter. Annabelle."

"Annabelle!" Olive gasped.

"Yes, Annabelle McMartin. And Annabelle was everything her grandfather could have hoped for: intelligent, greedy, and cruel."

Olive thought she might be sick. "Then, I guess . . . I did something terrible." Olive looked from Horatio to Harvey and back to Horatio. "I let her out. She said her name was Annabelle, and she was sad, and . . ." Olive trailed off, feeling exceptionally silly. "But I didn't know it was her! Annabelle is young and pretty, and Ms. McMartin was an old woman . . ."

"Well, she wasn't always old, you twit!" Horatio snapped.

"How dare you speak to a lady zat way!" demanded Harvey, looking ready to start a duel over whatever conflict was handy.

Olive stifled a frustrated scream. "Why didn't you warn me?"

"We *tried*!" Horatio exploded. "We gave you hint after hint! We told you to be careful if you went into the paintings. We told you not to bring things out. But we were forbidden to directly interfere with the McMartins' plans." Horatio's voice dropped, and a note of sadness trickled into it. "You know what we are, Olive. We belonged to them. We belong to their house."

"But zen you came along . . ." Harvey put in.

"Yes." Horatio sighed. "None of us thought you would discover so much so quickly, or that Annabelle's plans would come to pass. But you did, and they have. And if we don't want the McMartins controlling us again, we can't be cautious anymore."

"Oui," said Harvey. "Ze time has come for us to take a stand."

"But what does Annabelle want?!" Olive threw up her hands. "Why was she in a painting? Why do the paintings come to life? How did the people in the paintings get inside in the first place?"

"Keep your voice down," snapped Horatio. "Now

that things can't get much worse, I might as well tell you the whole story. Listen closely, and stop interrupting, if you possibly can." Horatio took a provoking pause, as if daring Olive to speak. Then, at last, he began:

"More than anything else, Aldous McMartin wanted to control life. He wanted to create it, trap it, make it last forever. First, he made the paintings—little worlds that could come to life if seen through a pair of enchanted spectacles. Because he had created the paintings, he had power over them. He could watch what went on inside, and use the paintings as windows, in a way, to keep an eye on the entire house. As he practiced, he got better and better at it. He painted portraits that could come to life, and that would even have the personalities of the people he had painted, but with one big improvement: These people could live forever. Sometimes he painted people as a reward, as he did for Annabelle. In her portrait, she would always be young and lovely, and she would always be loyal to him.

"Next, he learned to trap living people in paintings," said Horatio, pacing up and down the lip of the tub. "To make them *become* paintings. They weren't dead, exactly, but they weren't alive anymore either. They were . . . Elsewhere. That's what he did to the neighbors on Linden Street who knew too much about Old Man McMartin, as they called him. It's what he did to the builders who could have given away the secret of the gravestones, or to anyone else he disliked. Sometimes he just did it for fun. Like a collector pinning a living butterfly to a piece of cardboard."

In Olive's mind, the fragments of the story whirled and shifted. But this time, when they settled, she could see the whole picture. It had been there, in pieces, all along. "That was what he did to Morton," she breathed.

Horatio gave the tiniest nod.

"Morton was telling the truth. And I didn't believe him." The words felt as heavy as pebbles in her mouth. "He was alive. And you helped bring him here, and Aldous McMartin trapped him, and now . . . what?" Olive choked. "He's trapped forever? How could you do that to him?"

"Zat was the part I didn't like," said Harvey softly.

"Then why did you help Aldous McMartin?" demanded Olive furiously. "Why did you spy for him? Why did you trick innocent people?"

"We didn't have much choice!" retorted Horatio. "If you had ever been an indentured servant for a family of witches, you might begin to understand. Besides," the cat huffed, "we didn't always obey. After Aldous trapped the little boy from next door, I refused to help him anymore. Once, we even destroyed his paints and canvases."

"Oui. Zat was fun," said Harvey, gazing toward the ceiling and swiping his paw through an imaginary bit of cloth.

"But then he got that *dog* . . ." said Horatio.

"Baltus," hissed Harvey.

". . . and that helped Aldous keep us out of the way for a while. It took us years to get Baltus hidden away in that painting. And then you, Little Miss Rescue Crew, came along and let him out."

"Baltus!" Olive shouted so suddenly that both cats jumped. "I could hear Baltus even without the spectacles. And I could see Morton moving in the forest. The builders—their eyes glittered. And I noticed the necklace glinting in the lake before I put the spectacles on!" She looked from one cat to the other. "So the things that were from the real world . . . they still seem real in the paintings, even without the spectacles!"

"Very good," said Horatio, raising his whiskered eyebrows slightly. "Aldous never did get the things he'd taken from the real world to blend in completely."

"Wait a minute." Olive crossed her arms, frowning. "If he wanted to create eternal life, why didn't Aldous McMartin just paint a picture of himself?"

"He did," said Horatio.

"Dozens," said Harvey.

"His son destroyed them," Horatio continued. "Albert wasn't so stupid that he couldn't see what was going on. He lived in the same house, after all. He disliked the influence that his father was having over Annabelle, and finally he moved his wife and daughter out of this house and refused to let Annabelle see her grandfather, even though Annabelle was a young woman by that time and it was already far too late. However, Aldous decided to take care of that problem."

"How?" asked Olive. A creeping feeling tiptoed over her scalp.

"He killed Annabelle's parents," said Harvey bluntly.

"But there Aldous made a little mistake," said Horatio. "Annabelle was not as evil as her grandfather. After the murder of her mother and father, she began to realize that she did not want what her grandfather wanted. Maybe she didn't even *want* to live forever. Unfortunately, Aldous had planned for this, too." Horatio gave a significant look at the spot where the necklace hung against Olive's shirt. "Aldous was a very old man by this time. He painted one last self-portrait. And he put it in the locket that you are wearing at this very moment."

Olive clutched the pendant.

"Blackpaw's booty," whispered Harvey, a bit sadly, to the bathtub drain.

Horatio rolled his eyes.

"Aldous gave the necklace to his beloved granddaughter, and made her promise to bring him back to life by setting that portrait free," Horatio said. "Of course, by now, Annabelle had no intention of doing so. When Aldous did die at last, Annabelle had him cremated, so there would be no grave or gravestone, and she hid his ashes in a place she thought was safe. We've been helping her guard them for years. Then she tried to destroy the locket. But Aldous had made sure that Annabelle could never take it off. She wore it until she finally died of old age, at a hundred and four years old, right here in this house. And then this nincompoop in the tuna can breastplate made off with it before Leopold or I could find a safer spot for it." Horatio shot a look at Harvey, who was conveniently preoccupied with grooming his tail.

"Annabelle—Ms. McMartin—never had children, never told anyone her family's secrets," Horatio continued. "She wanted the McMartin line to end with her. Of course, it didn't really end. This house is still a powerful place. The painted version of Annabelle is wandering around, faithfully trying to bring her grandfather back. And you've got his picture hanging around your neck."

Olive clutched at the necklace. "What can we do?"

"My lady," Harvey proclaimed, "I have seen zee sorceress Annabelle moving through zee upstairs hallway.

She zhen entaired zee painting of zee street des Lindens, perhaps to get zee *petit garçon*. Zat means 'leetle boy.'"

"This will be much easier if you drop that accent," said Horatio.

Harvey glared.

"She has tried to get the necklace—and now she has gone to get the blood of a boy who cannot die to open it. All she needs . . ." Horatio trailed off.

The two cats gave each other a steady look. Then, in one smooth movement, they leaped out of the bathtub. Olive scrambled behind them. With Horatio and Harvey in the lead and Olive rushing blindly after, they ran down the stairs, into the kitchen, and through the creaking door of the basement.

EVENING HAD ENDED. It was night, dark and absolute. No light came in through the basement's high, small window but the faint white sheen of the moon. Like all cats, Harvey and Horatio could naturally see in the dark, and bounded down the stairs ahead of Olive. She trailed behind more slowly, keeping one hand on the wall, and trying to ignore the feeling of dread that trembled in the pit of her stomach.

The basement was as chilly and damp as usual. Olive's still-wet clothes clung to her clammily. She wished she were in a warm bathtub, or wrapped up in a blanket in front of a fire—in fact, she wished she were anywhere but a damp, dark basement with a trio of talking cats and a dangerous painted witch.

Horatio and Harvey moved soundlessly around the corner past the stairs. Olive tiptoed behind them as softly as she could, and almost stepped on Horatio's tail when both cats froze.

The flickering light of a candle broke the shadows in the corner. Olive saw Leopold's stalwart black bulk sitting at attention on the trapdoor. In front of him stood Annabelle.

Somehow Annabelle looked different already. Her carefully brushed hair had come out of its combs and hung in limp tangles against her back. Her face—or what Olive could see of it—looked sharper edged and cruel, not at all like the soft pink complexion from the portrait.

"Get out of the way, Leopold," Olive heard Annabelle snap.

"I'm afraid that's impossible, ma'am," answered Leopold, over a chest puffed out so grandiosely that it nearly eclipsed his chin.

"Very well," said Annabelle. "You'll move when I open the door."

Annabelle bent down to grasp the trapdoor's iron loop.

"A soldier doesn't like to hurt a lady, madam, but—" Leopold gave Annabelle a sharp swipe across the cheek.

Annabelle jerked back for a split second, looking

annoyed. Then she bent down toward the trapdoor again.

"Don't make me give you another," warned Leopold, but Annabelle brushed the cat off of the trapdoor with one powerful sideswipe. Leopold toppled backward, thrown against the stone wall.

Annabelle lifted the door and reached down into the dusty darkness. From inside, she hoisted out a smallish gold container that looked, to Olive, like something between a trophy and a lamp. It was covered with etched scrolls and curlicues, just like the patterns on the necklace around Olive's neck. Maybe she was imagining it, but Olive thought for a second that she could feel the metal of the necklace growing warm against her skin.

Annabelle turned, holding the urn in both hands, and spotted Horatio, Harvey, and Olive.

"Well, well. The gang's all here," said Annabelle, and Olive couldn't hear a trace of the sweet, polite voice of the Annabelle who had served her tea.

Harvey cleared his throat and puffed out his chest beneath his tin breastplate. "Lady, should you attempt to make away with those ashes, you shall face the righteous wrath of the guardians of this house," he proclaimed.

"Harvey, you deluded little mongrel," growled Annabelle. "I'd like to see what three cats and a dimwitted little girl could do to stop me."

Annabelle's eyes flicked over to Olive. "I see that you escaped from the lake," she said. "You must be feeling awfully proud of yourself. But it will only make things worse for you later." Candlelight flickered against the lifeless veneer of Annabelle's gold-brown eyes. "Then, I promise you, you'll wish you *had* drowned."

Annabelle lifted one hand from the urn and made a sign in the darkness. The pendant grew hot, burning Olive's skin. Olive tried to grab the chain, to lift the necklace away from her body, but found that she couldn't move a muscle. The pendant lay like a lump of burning coal against her chest.

With a twisted smile, Annabelle made a circular motion in the air. Olive spun in place. "There we are," said Annabelle. She glanced down at the cats. "If you wouldn't care for the same treatment," she warned, "I would suggest that you three make yourselves scarce."

Then, with a whisk of her long, filmy skirts, Annabelle set off for the stairs. Olive trailed behind her involuntarily, like a deflating balloon on a string.

Apparently, this was the last straw.

"*Charge!*" bellowed a voice from the darkness.

Olive saw a black blur fly through the air and plant itself firmly on Annabelle's shoulders. Another reddish blur tangled itself around her ankles.

"En garde!" yowled Harvey, before taking a flying leap and attaching himself to Annabelle's head like a furious Russian hat.

Annabelle gave a rather muffled shriek, since half of Harvey was covering her face. She batted and kicked at the cats, who clung as stubbornly as burs, reattaching their teeth and claws after each swipe. Still, despite the furor of her attackers, Annabelle trudged up the basement stairs with the urn clutched in her hand.

The whole hissing, howling group of them made it through the kitchen and into the hallway. Olive was dragged along behind them, with the necklace singeing a hole in her shirt. Her skin beneath it was blistered and sore. If the necklace had once been a magnet that pulled itself toward Olive, now it was a magnet that pulled Olive toward the urn in Annabelle's hands.

Annabelle made her way slowly up the stairs to the upper hallway, batting irritably at the cats. Horatio snaked between her ankles, trying to trip her, and Leopold slashed wildly at the urn, attempting to knock it out of Annabelle's iron grip. Harvey was still wrapped around her head. "Ye have met your match in King Arthur's knights, sorceress!" he cried. "The righteous shall prevail against evil!"

"Sad little lunatic," Annabelle muttered. Then she

raised one hand and snapped her fingers. The sound shot through the house like a whip-crack. It was followed by another sound: the creaking of a distant door.

"Baltus!" called Annabelle.

Out of the shadows of the attic thundered the gigantic dog. His paws beat the hallway carpet like sledgehammers. His long, yellow teeth were bared. He looked so different from the cheerful, tail-wagging mutt she had rescued from the painting that Olive almost didn't recognize him.

The three cats turned into hissing, bristled arches. The dog jumped, hallway light glinting on his wet teeth. Before Baltus's fangs could close around Horatio, who was still grappling with Annabelle's ankle, all three cats released their grip and zipped away down the staircase. The huge dog thundered after them. The sound of claws scrambling across polished hardwood faded into the distance.

Olive held her breath, listening for hissing, growling, or shouting—anything that would tell her the cats were still safe—but the house had gone silent.

She ached to run down the stairs and throw herself into the battle. But her legs wouldn't move. She couldn't even turn her head. The necklace hung, smoldering, against her chest, and Annabelle stood beside her, a smile that didn't reach her eyes twisting her mouth into a cruel, painted hook.

Annabelle put on the spectacles. "We're going to visit your little friend," she said. Then she clamped her hand around Olive's wrist. Together they climbed into the painting of the dark forest.

THE COLD WIND rippled through Olive's hair. For the first time, she felt thankful for the icy forest air, for the slight relief it gave to her sore skin beneath the searing pendant.

Annabelle darted quickly, almost running, down the white path through the trees. Olive trailed after her, unable even to push away the thorny branches that slashed her face and arms. The moon seemed to grow dimmer and more distant as they followed the path into the heart of the forest.

At last they came to a clearing. Here, the thick trees and underbrush had been swept away, leaving a hole for the pale moonlight to fill. The white path broke into two halves, forming a perfect circle around one stump. Sunk deep into the wood of the stump glittered something that looked, to Olive, like the hilt of a dagger.

There was a soft whimpering from one side of the clearing. Olive couldn't turn her head, but forced her eyes in the direction of the familiar sound. She spotted Morton, still wearing his oversized nightshirt, tied to a small bare tree. Olive's whole body itched with frustration. She wanted to run to him, but she couldn't even speak.

Annabelle set the urn gently on the smooth surface of the stump. Now with both hands free, she crossed the clearing and untied Morton, although Olive noticed that Morton's little ankles were still bound together, so that he nearly had to hop as Annabelle hustled him back to the stump.

Morton's round, terrified face looked up at Olive. Olive, who couldn't move anything else, gave Morton the biggest wink she could manage.

Slowly, Annabelle removed the lid from the urn. In the moonlight, her face was twisted and cruel, her eyes like little oil fires. Olive couldn't believe she'd ever found Annabelle beautiful.

"Hold out your hand, boy," said Annabelle to Morton.

Morton froze, too terrified to move. Olive thought of the rabbits she had seen in the backyard, who seemed to imagine that motionlessness made them invisible.

Unfortunately, this didn't work for Morton any better than it worked for the rabbits.

Annabelle grabbed Morton's arm roughly, and he let out a frightened peep. She turned his little hand palm-up over the open urn.

"Come closer, Olive," Annabelle whispered. Olive's feet shuffled nearer to the stump, even while her brain commanded them not to.

Annabelle reached out and grasped the pendant that hung around Olive's neck, dragging Olive down to the urn. Then she yanked the dagger out of the stump. Moonlight flashed on its sharp blade as Annabelle dragged the knife swiftly across Morton's palm. Drops of blood or paint, black in the darkness, fell over the gold metal of the locket and into the urn's open mouth. With the point of the dagger, Annabelle wedged open the filigreed halves of the pendant. Olive heard the click of a tiny hinge.

Inside the locket was a portrait. Even though the painting was upside-down, Olive could make out a face—a bony, angular face with deep pits for eyes and a sharp, square jaw. She recognized it instantly. It was the man from the old photograph she found in the back of the chest of drawers.

"Come out, Grandfather," Annabelle said. Slowly, like smoke, the image in the portrait slithered out of the locket toward the open mouth of the urn. Annabelle bowed her head. "I have kept my promise to you," she whispered. "This is still our house. It will always be ours, and no one will ever again chase our family away."

Olive glanced at Morton from the corner of her eye. He was staring down, mouth agape, squeezing his hand. The cut had vanished.

Annabelle lifted the urn above her head. Its gold body flashed in the moonlight. A sudden wind rose, knocking Olive and Morton off of their feet. Olive managed to catch herself, and realized that her body was once again doing what she told it to. The necklace hung cold and heavy against her shirt. Morton scrambled toward her. She wrapped her arms tightly around his skinny shoulders, and this time Morton didn't shrug her arms away.

The black trees bent wildly in the wind. Bits of dead leaves and twigs whipped through the chilly air. Olive squinted up into the fading light to see that Annabelle was laughing, holding the urn high. A trail of ashes coiled from the urn's mouth. As Olive watched, the rising ashes grew thicker, darker, spinning through the air. They eclipsed the moon. They filled the sky. They muffled Annabelle's triumphant laugh with the sound of a swirling, papery storm.

Pulling Morton along beside her, Olive crawled toward the edge of the clearing. The cycling wind

sucked at them, trying to pull them back. Head down, Olive fought her way out into the trees, moving into a crouch, and then a run.

"Wait!" called Morton, who was hopping after her as fast as he could, his ankles still bound together. Behind him, the ashes scythed through the trees like the wings of a million black insects. The sound alone made Olive's skin crawl.

She scrambled back toward Morton. With shaking, freezing hands, she managed to slip one of his bare feet out of the rope. Together they scuttled onto the white path just ahead of the swirling ashes.

"Hurry!" Olive yelled. "Run! If we can get to the picture frame, we can call for help!"

Morton tucked his chin to his chest and pumped his little legs as fast as he possibly could. Olive raced along beside him, holding tight to his hand.

The wind struck at them like leather whips. Olive's hair flew in every direction, into her mouth, into her eyes. They had come to the end of the path, but the sky was getting darker, colder. Dead grass lashed wildly around their ankles. The frame, with its picture of the hallway, glowed dimly ahead of them.

"Horatio!" Olive screamed. "Leopold! Harvey!"

"Help us!" yelled Morton.

Still running, Olive looked up at the spot where the moon used to be. In the dark clouds of ash, she was sure she could make out a face—an angular face, with pits where eyes should have been. It roiled and spread, blotting out all but the faintest glow of moonlight.

Olive turned back toward the frame a moment too late. A long black tree branch swung out across the path, thwacking her in the stomach. She landed on her back, dragging Morton along with such force that he did a backward somersault.

Olive flipped over onto her hands and knees. "Follow me, and stay low!" she commanded. They scrambled off the path into the thick underbrush. "If we can just wait long enough, I'm sure Horatio will come for us. I'm sure he will."

Morton nodded, squinting in the wind.

"Here—this is a good spot," Olive whispered as they crawled into a cluster of massive tree trunks. "Let's just stay hidden and wait."

Morton squeezed close to Olive, and they both wriggled down against the roots of the trees. "I told you I was real," he whispered. "I have blood. You saw it."

"I know," Olive answered. "I know." She thought of the silence where Morton's heartbeat should have been. The blood that might actually have been paint. *You were real once,* she thought to herself. Aloud, she only said, "I'm sorry I didn't believe you."

Morton nodded, looking down at his bare toes.

Olive smoothed out the rumples in his nightshirt, making sure it covered his legs. Then they were quiet for a moment, leaning against each other.

Olive tried sending out a mental distress signal to Horatio. Sometimes people in stories did that. *Come and get us,* she thought. Then, just because she knew how much Horatio would hate it, she thought, *Here, kitty, kitty, kitty*, and had to swallow an insane giggle.

Something behind them moved. Olive could feel it shifting in the ground. It trailed over her arm, and when she looked down, one tree root had snaked out of the dirt and was wrapping itself around her wrist. She gasped, scuttling away. Another branch reached toward her. She dodged before it could coil around her neck. Morton was kicking at the roots that were trying to bind his ankles.

"Get up!" shouted Olive, slapping at the branches. "We have to move! It's Annabelle—she's trying to trap us!"

Dodging out of the underbrush, Morton and Olive ran back onto the clear space of the path. "The cats might not hear us. They might not be able to help us," Olive puffed to Morton. "But if they don't, nobody will know where we are, and then *neither* of us will ever see our families . . ." A sob squeezed down on Olive's voice.

She pictured her parents coming home and finding the house empty. They would panic and cry and call the police, never knowing that their daughter was stuck on the other side of a picture frame at the top of the hallway stairs. Morton's parents had probably done the very same thing, years and years ago, never guessing that their little boy was right next door, waiting to be found before it was too late. But nobody did find him. And now it *was* too late.

No.

Olive stopped so suddenly that Morton almost crashed into her.

No. NO. It wasn't too late. She wouldn't let it be too late. Morton had been stuck in this painting before, but she wasn't going to let it happen to him again. She wasn't going to let it happen to her.

Morton gaped up at her. "What? What? Why are we stopping?"

Olive made her voice as steady as she could. "Morton, we can't wait for the cats. We have to get those spectacles. If we can take them and get out, then Annabelle will be stuck in here for good."

Morton cringed, looking past Olive into the trees. "Look," he whispered, pointing. From where they stood, they could just glimpse Annabelle through the trees, the pastels of her trailing skirts pale against the black silhouettes. They had run almost all the way back to the clearing.

Olive and Morton slunk closer, keeping as quiet as they could while dodging and fighting off the branches that grabbed at them. They stopped at the edge of the clearing and huddled between the trunks.

"We should split up," Olive whispered to Morton. She jerked her arm away from a persistent branch and glanced toward the sky. The swirling clouds were thickening, pulling together into a huge, spinning funnel. The face Olive had seen—if it was still there, and she felt sure that it was—seemed to be lost in the churning dark. "Something is happening. I'm not sure how much time we'll have."

"Right." Morton nodded, his moony head bouncing like a bobble-head doll on a dashboard. "I'll distract her. You get the spectacles."

Olive stared hard at Morton for a moment. Something intent and solemn had settled over the fear on his face, like a cloak, hiding everything but its faint outline. "All right," she whispered. "Be careful."

Morton nodded once more. Then he tripped on the hem of his nightshirt and stumbled away to the right.

Olive crouched, squinting into the clearing. Annabelle was walking around and around the stump, mumbling something to herself and making signs in the air. Olive could see the spectacles hanging around Annabelle's neck. Her heart gave a hopeful little bounce.

A thin branch coiled around Olive's leg and she

kicked at it distractedly. The branch snapped, and quickly mended its broken halves. In the clearing, Annabelle froze.

Just then, Morton charged into the open, still tugging at something strapped to his leg. Olive squinted, trying to see through the darkness. In Morton's fist was the little flashlight Olive had brought him.

"Ta-DA!" he sang. He flicked on the light. A tiny, cheerful streak of gold bobbed around the clearing like a firefly.

But it was too late. Annabelle had spotted Olive.

"Hey, lady," Morton shouted. "Over here! Look!" Morton pointed the flashlight toward the dark sky. The clouds swirled and broke, pulling away from its beam.

Annabelle ignored him. She turned toward Olive with a sickening smile and gestured with both hands. The trees around Olive sprang to life. Roots knotted around her ankles. Branches locked her arms tight against her sides. Another branch wrapped itself around her neck and began to squeeze. Olive felt her face start to tingle.

"The old man doesn't like this! You'd better come over here and stop me!" she heard Morton shouting in the distance.

Olive couldn't breathe. Little fireworks exploded in front of her eyes. Through them, she could see Annabelle moving closer, the spectacles glinting on their chain. In the distance, a little white shape darted forward. Something gleamed through the darkness.

"YAH!" Morton yowled, leaping forward and landing on Annabelle's trailing skirts, pinning her to the ground. Annabelle whirled around. The beam of Morton's flashlight struck her full in the face. Annabelle let out a shriek and raised her arms, shielding her eyes from the light.

All at once, the branches around Olive's body loosened. With a wriggle, she slipped out of their grasp and charged through the trees into the clearing, throwing herself against Annabelle's back. Morton still had the flashlight aimed at Annabelle's eyes. "YAH!" he shouted again. Annabelle covered her face with one arm and flailed blindly at Morton with the other.

"Grandfather!" Annabelle yelled toward the sky.

Olive felt her fist close around the spectacles and yanked backward with all the strength in her body. The chain snapped. The spectacles were secure in her hand.

"Come on!" Olive shouted, grabbing Morton's arm.

They bolted down the path, the beam of Morton's flashlight bobbing wildly over the ground in front of them. Its light was already getting weaker. "I think the batter is draining out!" gasped Morton.

Another pair of running footsteps joined the sound

of their own. Olive glanced over her shoulder. Annabelle was after them, the dagger she had used to cut Morton clasped in her fist.

Olive put on the spectacles. "When we get to the frame," she panted to Morton, "you go first. I'll be right behind you."

The small square of hallway light shone just a few steps in front of them. Olive pushed Morton ahead. He grabbed the bottom of the frame, Olive held him by the ankle, and Morton dove out into the hallway.

Annabelle lunged closer, her hands reaching out, her mouth forming a furious NO. Willing herself not to look back, Olive grasped the frame. She heaved her body over it, pushing her head and shoulders out into the gold light of the hallway. But she couldn't get any farther. Annabelle's hand was locked around her foot.

Olive kicked wildly, her legs hitting nothing but the cold, swirling air of the forest. Then there was a sudden tug, and the sensation of something slipping away. Her left sock was gone. Her foot was free of Annabelle's grasp. Annabelle stumbled backward, still clutching Olive's stripy sock, and Olive toppled out into the hallway.

She landed on her stomach on the hall carpet. Morton sat in exhausted silence beside her. Then his eyes grew wide. He looked at Olive. "We did it," he said. He scrambled to his feet. "We did it! We did it!"

he chanted, hopping up and down, waving the dead flashlight.

Something sharp was poking Olive in the ribs, but she didn't seem to be bleeding, and she knew it wasn't Annabelle's knife. She felt around cautiously with one hand.

Broken glass.

Olive jerked upright, grasping the bent wire that still dangled from the chain around her neck. She had landed on the spectacles.

"Uh-oh," said Morton softly.

"I know," said Olive. "I broke them. I break everything."

"Look," whispered Morton.

Olive glanced up, following Morton's eyes. In the frame where the painted forest should have been, a black cloud was pouring out into the hallway. It ran over the bottom edge of the frame like a dark waterfall. It gathered into a pool, and then the pool began to grow higher, thicker, larger, until it was a pillar that nearly reached the ceiling. There was a body in the pillar. A tall, gaunt body, with a rigid face, and deep pits where eyes should have been. It towered over them in a whirl of ashes. The pits of the eyes stared down at Morton and Olive. Then the air turned to ice, and the lights went out.

20

OLIVE HUDDLED, SHIVERING, in the darkness. She couldn't see Morton cowering beside her. She couldn't even see her hands when she waved them in front of her face. The windows at the end of the hall were dark, without a single tiny star poking through the night. Once, Olive had visited a cave on a school field trip. The tour guide had stopped them in one narrow little chamber, deep underground, and turned out the lights. In that moment, Olive had felt just what she felt now—absolute darkness, icy, damp, and complete.

Something brushed her arm. Olive jumped.

"Olive?" said a very tiny whisper.

"I'm here," Olive whispered back.

Morton groped for her hand. "I just thought you might be scared."

"I'm going to find the light switch," said Olive as bravely as she could.

With Morton beside her, Olive groped along the hallway walls until her fingers brushed the switch. She flicked it up and down. Nothing happened.

"Let's try another one," said Olive stubbornly. She reached through her own bedroom door, running her palm up and down the wall. She clicked the switch. Nothing.

Olive's teeth were starting to chatter. The air was as cold as the inside of a refrigerator.

"I'm going to find some candles," she told Morton. "Keep right next to me."

"You keep right next to *me*," said Morton.

Her body pressed to the wall, Olive sidled toward one of the upstairs bathrooms. There on the countertop were two scented candles in little glass jars. Olive ran her hands over the counter until she found the matchbook. She struck a match. A bright yellow flame flared in her hand, and in the bathroom mirror, her own reflection stared back above another bobbing yellow flame. The darkness pulled back, very slightly, but she could feel something icy breathing on her neck—something that didn't like the light.

Olive and Morton each carried a lit candle out into the hallway. Olive could see her breath in the air. Her clothes, still damp from the lake, were now freezing.

Olive held her candle up to the paintings along the hall. They had all turned black, as though someone had doused the canvases with dark paint.

Moving very carefully down the stairs, holding up her cinnamon-scented candle, Olive could feel the darkness close around them. She could hear it breathing. It lifted the strands of her hair and tugged on the cuffs of her jeans. Olive shuddered. There was something *in* the darkness—something with a human shape, but something that hadn't been human for more than a hundred years.

She reached the foot of the stairs, with Morton right behind her. Something that felt like long, cold fingers trailed across the back of her neck.

"Was that you, Morton?" she breathed.

"Was that me what?" Morton whispered back.

"*Olive . . .*" murmured a voice in the darkness.

"Olive?" said a very different voice.

The darkness pulled back a little more. The air thawed by a few degrees. Olive glanced around. Three pairs of bright green eyes glittered in the light of her candle.

"Horatio! Leopold! Harvey!" Olive felt as if she might collapse from relief. The cats encircled her feet, staring out protectively into the darkness like three feline gargoyles. "What happened to the dog?" she whispered.

Horatio jerked his head toward the basement door,

where there was the sound of petulant whining and scratching. "Good old Baltus," said Horatio sarcastically.

"Old Man Mc—I mean Aldous McMartin," Olive stammered, "Aldous McMartin is here. He got out."

"Affirmative," said Leopold. "We know."

"He wants to get rid of you, Olive," said Horatio.

"You mean—?"

"Kill you. Yes. Or trap you." Horatio turned to look up into Olive's face. "The sooner the better, as far as he's concerned. He wants his house back. He and Annabelle were the last of the McMartins, and they won't let their legacy end so easily."

Olive's candle sputtered. "What will he do to me?" she whispered.

"Well," said Horatio, "the easiest way would be to put you into a painting and leave you there forever, like your friend there."

Olive heard Morton suck in his breath.

"Or he might do something quicker, more permanent. Like he did to Albert," said Leopold.

"*Hwwwckkk*," said Harvey helpfully, running one paw across his throat.

"He will try to control you, Olive," said Horatio. "He's been watching you. He knows you. He'll use the things you want and the things you fear. He will threaten whatever you care about most."

Olive swallowed hard. She glanced around at the

dark rooms full of her parents' books and shoes and papers, at the three cats staring up at her expectantly, at Morton's pale form wavering in the dim light, and she could feel it all slipping away from her. She had wanted these things to be hers. She had even started to believe that she belonged here, and that the house belonged to her family, and that they would stay in one spot for good. But this house wasn't hers. She was going to be turned away again.

"I deserve this," Olive whispered. "This is all my fault anyway. I found the necklace. I let Annabelle out. I put everybody in danger."

"Do not think it, my lady!" Harvey dismissed Olive's words with a grand wave of his paw. "It would have happened with or without you."

"For once, he's right," said Horatio. "They used you. You were necessary, for a while. Now . . . you are only in the way." His eyes flicked to the nightshirt-draped figure behind her. "Like Morton was, once. Like Mr. McMartin's son. Like his neighbors."

"Like us," added Leopold softly.

Realization washed over Olive like a cold tide. Of course. Aldous McMartin would punish the cats for betraying him. He would have plans for Morton, too—that was certain. And tomorrow morning, when her parents came home . . . Olive shook her head violently, forcing these visions away.

And then, in her chest, something flared to life, like a match touching a candle's wick. Suddenly Olive wasn't scared. She was *angry*.

Olive squared her shoulders and took a deep breath. Her exhalation made a long gold plume of smoke. She looked around at the walls of the house, flickering with shadows and fragile light. She looked down at the cats' glittering green eyes. If she could stop him—*when* she stopped him—Old Man McMartin could never have power over any of them again.

"I'm not going to let the McMartins get rid of us," she said slowly. "I'm going to get rid of *them*."

Harvey let out a whoop and performed a triumphant jig on the steps. Leopold gave a military nod so sharp it could have cut a steak, and Horatio actually rubbed his head against Olive's ankles and began to purr, before he caught himself.

"So, what do we do?" Olive asked.

Horatio, Leopold, and Harvey looked at one another, and then up at Olive, their green eyes glowing like small flames. Horatio said slowly, "To get rid of the shadows, you'll need to bring the light."

"Morton will help, too. Won't you, Morton?"

But there was no answer. Morton wasn't there.

OLIVE RAIDED THE kitchen cupboards for matches, flashlights, and camping lanterns. Her hands shook with fear, which made them even clumsier than usual. "I think you hurt Morton's feelings, talking about what Aldous McMartin might do," Olive fumed at the cats, knocking down an old coffeepot that nearly landed on Harvey's head. "'Stick you in a painting and leave you there forever.' Very sensitive, guys. Now he could be anywhere in the house—if Old Man McMartin hasn't trapped him somewhere already." Olive bit her lip, picturing Morton lost inside some strange painting, all alone once again.

"We'll find him, miss," Leopold declared. "But we must proceed with caution. A soldier doesn't run into battle unarmed."

Olive huffed and turned back to the kitchen shelves.

It was dark, chilly work, and her fingers were growing numb. Patches of her damp clothes were covered with frost. The cats, who could see in the dark and who didn't seem to be bothered by the temperature, stayed close to Olive's feet, their bright eyes scanning the darkness.

The shadows and the cold and her worry for Morton were wearing Olive down. Her arms and legs felt heavy; her toes had apparently disappeared. Her eyelids were so, so heavy. All she wanted was to lie down on the floor and go to sleep. Sleep would be warm and comfortable, and safe . . .

Something sharp dug into her ankle.

Olive looked down to see Horatio glaring up. "Don't close your eyes," he said sternly. "Keep moving."

Olive stuck a spare flashlight into her pocket. She hung the large camping lantern over her arm and clutched one more flashlight in her free hand.

"I'm not sure how long these batteries will last," said Olive, turning on the first flashlight.

"We will have to work quickly," agreed Horatio. "The longer he is here, in his house, the stronger he grows."

"We'll search each room, starting on the first floor," commanded Leopold, clearly in his element. "Don't waste the batteries. Wait until you have gotten a clear look at him before you hit him with the beam."

Harvey, Horatio, and Olive nodded.

"Forward march!" Leopold announced.

By the glow of Olive's small flashlight, they set out along the hall.

The shadows that slid away from them were not ordinary household shadows. They looked like silhouettes—distorted, enlarged outlines of people scuttling across the dim walls. "Morton?" Olive called. No one answered. Olive and the cats' own shadows moved tentatively through the hall, trailing wisps of steam in the chilly air.

In the library, Olive ran her flashlight over the bookshelves. The beam of dim light glinted as it struck the embossed covers and the intricate swirls of the chandelier, cutting a muted hole in the darkness. It reminded Olive of the movies she had seen of explorers searching through sunken ships. With the icy cold and the solid dark, the house could have been a mile deep under the ocean.

"The old man is here," whispered Horatio.

Something moved past them in the darkness. Olive felt it brush the bare skin of her arm. It felt wet, and cold, and dead—like an eel, or a strip of seaweed, or like a bedsheet that has been left hanging in the freezing rain. Olive tried to trace it with the flashlight. It was too late; already the figure in the darkness had slipped past them, out the library door.

There was a sudden, high-pitched scream from above.

"Morton!" gasped Olive.

Olive and the cats clambered toward the stairs, Harvey and Leopold racing with each other to see who would go protectively in the lead.

"Three o'clock, men!" shouted Leopold.

"If you mean it came from the right, just say so," snapped Horatio.

Harvey was the first to make it through the door to Olive's bedroom, with Leopold tripping over him, and Olive tripping over them both.

The scent of candle smoke hung in the air. Olive tightened her grip on the flashlight. "Morton?"

There was no answer. She swept the beam across the room. On her bed, the sheets lay in a twisted tangle, the covers had slipped to one side, and one of the pillows had fallen to the floor. Hershel lay on his back in the center of the bed, looking stunned.

"Morton? Are you here?" whispered Olive.

"Down here," said Horatio, his tail poking out from beneath the dust ruffle.

Olive got down on her hands and knees and aimed the flashlight under the bed. Morton was curled up beneath the mattresses in his usual defense position: a tight, nightshirt-swaddled ball. He blinked, wide-eyed, into the light.

"Olive?" he whispered. "That light hurts my eyes."

"Sorry," said Olive, aiming the flashlight away. "Are you all right?"

"I came up here to fight him," said Morton, in the toughest voice a boy hiding under a bed can manage.

"By yourself?"

"I'm strong. I can do it. See?" Morton made a fist and rolled up the sleeve over one spaghetti noodle-ish arm. There was a moment of silence. Then Olive nudged Harvey and Leopold, who made impressed, supportive noises.

Morton wiggled to the side of the bed. "He was in here," Morton said. "He put out the candle. It got so dark, and he came after me. Then he told me to close my eyes and go to sleep. I didn't want to do it. But he was making me do it. Just like—just like before." He looked at them and swallowed. "And then it got even darker, and I screamed, and then you came."

Morton looked up at Olive, his breath making puffs of steam in the dark air. "I want to go home," he said. "My REAL home." His lip wobbled precariously.

"I know," said Olive. "We're trying," she added, because trying was all she could promise. She brushed a small dust bunny off Morton's sleeve.

"Whither did the villain go?" snarled Harvey, running one claw demonstratively over the leg of the bed.

"Let me see but his shadow, and I will show you a duel that time will not soon forget!"

"You can't see anything *but* his shadow, you nitwit," snapped Horatio.

"Men, this is no time for quarreling." Leopold hopped up onto the bed and marched along the edge of the mattress, gazing down at his troops. "This is a time for action. The first question is: Where did he go?"

"I don't think he went anywhere," said Morton, pulling the askew blankets down around him like a cape. Hershel plopped down onto the floorboards.

Harvey sniffed the air. "The lad speaks aright," he whispered.

Olive let the beam of her flashlight run slowly over the walls. Shadows swirled and thinned in the corners, trailing bony arms along the edges of the light. Something that looked like a long, twisted hand beckoned with one lumpy finger. The flashlight beam was growing dim.

"I think these batteries are dying," said Olive. As they watched, the light became fuzzy and thin. Then it deepened slowly into black, fading out like the last image on a movie screen.

As Olive scrambled to pull a fresh flashlight out of her pocket, Morton gave a terrified peep. Leopold jumped down onto her shoulders. Horatio and Harvey arched their backs, hissing. Blackness fell over them like a blanket.

Again, Olive felt the cold, wet touch of the shadows. They trailed over her bare arms, brushed her face. And this time, they held on.

Olive tried to reach for the flashlight but her arms were being held tight. Long, dark fingers had wrapped like cables around her wrists. She felt a cold breath brush her cheek, and she was sure it wasn't Leopold's. "*Olive . . .*" a voice whispered.

"Be gone, fiend!" yowled Harvey, leaping into the darkness. Horatio jumped after him. The shadows retreated for just a moment. Olive used that split second to get a firm grip on the backup flashlight in her right pocket. She sliced the beam through the darkness like a sword.

Harvey was lying on his back with all four claws in midair. Leopold was sitting up on his two hind legs with his forepaws posed like a boxer. Horatio had positioned himself defensively, teeth bared, on Morton's lap. The three cats froze in their positions as a clot of shadows slithered swiftly around the edge of the door.

"There he goes!" shouted Leopold, bounding toward the hallway. "Harvey, guard the boy!" Harvey made a pouting sound, which Leopold ignored. "Miss, bring the lantern! Hurry! We'll guard your flank—he's heading for the attic!"

"I'm coming too!" shouted Morton. "Somebody give me a lantern!"

Olive scrambled to her feet, gripping the handle of the camp lantern in her left hand and the flashlight in her right. Horatio and Leopold ran at her heels. Behind them came Morton and Harvey, looking for something to light Morton's candle. Olive skidded into the hallway, raced to the front bedroom, and stopped in front of the huge gold frame. The ancient town, like every other painting, had gone dark. Only the huge stone arch remained on the canvas, its stern-faced soldiers staring down from either side. But now, at the end of its massive stone tunnel, there was only blackness.

"The spectacles—" moaned Olive. "I can't get through."

"I'll take you, miss," said Leopold.

"It would be a privilege, my lady," said Harvey, bolting into the room and bumping Leopold aside.

"I'll take you, but I'm not sure what will happen if we go through a painting that looks like this," said Horatio.

For a moment, all of them stared through the stone archway into the darkness.

"We have to try it anyway," said Olive. "Let's all go."

Olive grabbed Horatio's tail in one hand and Leopold's in the other. Morton, unlit candle still clamped in one fist, took hold of Harvey's tail with his free hand. Together, they all stepped through the archway, and beyond the frame.

It was like passing through a waterfall. In a blink, the darkness washed over them, cold and heavy. Then they were all standing in the tiny, dusty entry to the attic. Olive let go of the cats' tails and groped for the doorknob.

A blast of freezing air hit her face. Olive didn't hesitate. She was already on the first stair when something knocked the flashlight out of her hand. The attic door slammed shut behind her, leaving her all alone.

OLIVE COULD HEAR the cats scratching furiously at the other side of the door. She groped for the doorknob and pulled, but the door was stuck firmly shut. It was as if the entire weight of the darkness were pressing against it, sealing it closed.

"Morton!" she called, tugging wildly at the door. "Horatio!"

If anyone gave an answer, Olive couldn't hear it.

Olive groped along the dusty steps for her dropped flashlight, but it was nowhere to be found. It was as if it had been swallowed by the darkness. She pulled out the flashlight that was still wedged in her left pocket. It was a smallish light, the kind people keep in their glove compartments in case they have to change a tire in the dark. Olive wished that she were only changing a tire. She had no idea how it was done, but she was sure that it would be easier than this.

Cautiously, she moved the light back and forth along each step of the attic stairs. Spiders skittered out of the beam. Other bugs—dead ones—littered the steps. Olive would normally have minded the dead bugs just as much as the living ones, but she realized that at the moment, bugs—even dead ones—seemed positively friendly.

The attic smelled, as before, of dust and old paper, but now the smell was fainter, dulled by the freezing cold. The stairs creaked under her feet. She climbed carefully, twitching the beam of light back and forth,

Olive reached the top of the stairs and looked around. The lumpy shapes of covered furniture and jumbled boxes made vague mounds in the darkness. She ran the small white circle of her flashlight around the room.

The darkness played tricks with her eyes, making the piled shape of an old armoire look like someone looming in the shadows, and turning the hat rack into a leering skeleton. Olive could hear her own heart thundering in her ears. She wished that something—anything—would break the menacing silence.

So she cleared her throat and started to sing.

Olive wasn't a very good singer, but she was a very

loud singer. She began with "This Little Light of Mine," and moved on to "Let the Sun Shine In." Then she sang as many verses of "Candle on the Water" as she could remember, which wasn't very many, so she sang the refrain five or six times. As long as she was singing, Olive felt just the teeniest bit less alone.

The darkness seemed to be listening. Olive edged slowly around the attic, peering into the clutter with her flashlight. As she moved, the shadows on the slanted walls flickered and twisted like black smoke.

She was singing the only words she could remember from "Glow, Little Glowworm" when the beam of her flashlight sputtered and went out. "Glitter, glitter . . ." Her voice wavered and faded away like the beam of light.

Olive's hand quivered. She heard the flashlight fall from her fingers and thump on the floor. The light had been too small to do any real good, of course. She might as well have tried to fight a duel with a toothpick. But it had been comforting. The camping lantern still dangled from her other hand. It was her last chance. She knew she had to save it.

Something moved in the dark behind her. She felt a cold touch on her neck. Olive spun around. There was nothing there. At least, nothing that she could see.

The cold came from every direction. The shadows grew thicker and thicker. They reminded Olive of thunderclouds, pulling themselves together into huge piles before a storm.

And then Olive felt something filmy and cold run over her arm. A scream moved up her throat and tried to get out of her mouth, but it ran into her clenched teeth and came out of her nose instead. Olive bolted toward the stairs. Halfway there, she remembered that the door was stuck shut. And, on the other side of that door, Morton, Horatio, Leopold, and Harvey were waiting. They were probably listening, with all of their ears pressed to the door. They would hear her running down the stairs, giving up.

Olive stopped. She turned slowly back toward the center of the attic.

"I'm not afraid of you," she said to the darkness. Her voice sounded weak and quivery. Olive took a deep breath and said it again. "I'm not afraid of you, Mr. Aldous McMartin! And I don't think you're such a great painter, either!"

This time her words filled up the whole attic. For a moment, the darkness pulled back. Then it rushed toward her, wrapping itself around her body, freezing against her bare skin. Olive's arms and legs felt full of lead.

Her teeth were chattering, but she said as lightly as she could, "Is that supposed to be scary? Because it isn't."

She shuffled toward the center of the attic, rubbing her freezing arms with her hands. Her toe bumped something tall and wooden, which creaked on its hinges. Olive reached out one tentative palm. It was a mirror—the old, floor-length, tilting kind. And with that, the little twinkling seed of a plan rooted itself in Olive's mind.

She worked quickly. The attic was freezing, its cold air stinging her throat and lungs, but Olive forced herself to keep moving. Even though it was still much too dark to see, her other senses were adjusting. She had never heard things so sharply and clearly; she had never realized how much her fingertips could tell her. Olive whipped the dusty sheets off of the old furniture, running her hands quickly over their surfaces, dragging things into place.

At first, she thought she was imagining it when strange things began to appear in the darkness. She knew that when you stared at a light and then closed your eyes, you could still see its traces on the inside of your eyelids. If you pushed your fingers against your closed eyes, sometimes spots of color jumped and flashed against the blackness, like Christmas lights stuck through black paper. So maybe it was only her eyes playing tricks when a long, eely shape moved through the darkness and flickered past her face. That was what Olive told herself. She told herself the same thing when something with wide, staring eyes and long teeth swam through the corner of her vision. But when something slippery and cold and covered with scales dragged itself slowly across her ankles, Olive knew that it wasn't her imagination.

She wished that she could reach out and flick a light switch. But she couldn't. She was having a nightmare, and she couldn't wake up.

In spite of the cold, beads of sweat popped up like a rash on Olive's bare skin. She rubbed her arms, holding herself tightly. For a moment, she felt so forlorn that she wanted to lie down on the floor and cry. She would probably fall asleep and get hypothermia, she knew, but at least all of this would be over. No more cold snaky things with big eyes and teeth slithering past her through the black.

"That's just what you want, isn't it?" Olive whispered to the darkness.

No one answered.

Olive kicked both her feet. There was nothing there—at least, not anymore. She took a shaky breath and got back to work.

More grayish shapes with long, whipping tails swam around her. Some shapes had beaks, long noses, claws that sliced through the dark air. Olive ignored them, or pretended to. They were only a distraction, an illusion. The real danger was still lurking in the darkness, not yet allowing itself to be seen. She went back to humming "Let the Sun Shine In" as carelessly as she could, pushing the furniture into position.

It was getting harder to ignore the cold, however. Her whole body was shaking so badly that she was afraid she was going to knock something over. Her toes, especially the ones on her bare foot, were as lifeless as pebbles. She couldn't even feel the cold in them anymore. Her fingers were so stiff and numb, she was afraid they might shatter. The armoire rattled as she hauled it slowly toward the center of the attic. Olive knew that she wouldn't be able to keep going for much longer. Her eyelashes were freezing together, coated by the quickly cooling steam of her breath.

Finally, all of the pieces were in place. Olive pulled an old footstool into the very center of the attic, held the camping lantern in her lap, and waited.

It was hard to sit still. The cold was ten times worse the moment she stopped moving, and the darkness was gathering itself. It settled around her, as solid as stone. Olive began to have the feeling that she wouldn't be able to move if she tried.

"Olive," said a voice. It was no longer a whisper. Now it was a low, solid voice—a man's voice. It sounded like rocks grinding against one another in a very deep, dark hole. "Olive, come with me."

Olive's foot twitched. "No," she whispered.

"Come here," commanded the voice.

Both of Olive's feet made a little shuffling step. "No," Olive said, more loudly this time. "I'm not going to go with you and let you push me out a window."

In the darkness behind her, a man laughed. "Very well. I simply thought you would want to get away from those spiders."

She felt them first on her ankles, and then on her calves, and then everywhere on her body: hundreds of running legs—legs skittering and crawling and climbing all over her. Olive squeezed her eyes shut. If she screamed, they would go into her mouth. More than anything, she wanted to turn on the lantern and prove that the spiders were only a trick, but if she did, her whole plan would be spoiled. It was her last chance.

This isn't real, Olive told herself. *This isn't real this isn't real this isn't real.*

All at once, the tickling, crawling legs were gone. Olive took a deep breath.

"You're a brave girl, Olive," said the voice. "That's one of your few good qualities, isn't it?"

Olive's stomach gave a sick little lurch.

The voice went on, lower, closer. "Your parents will wonder where you've gone. For a while, that is. Eventually they'll move on. Perhaps they will have another child. One that is more . . . what they had hoped for." The voice sighed. "I know—children can be such a terrible disappointment sometimes."

Olive forced her voice out of her throat. "They wouldn't forget me. They'd look for me."

"But is there anyone else who will?" the voice rumbled against Olive's neck. When she turned around, no one was there. The voice went on. "Is there anyone else, in all the world, who will truly miss you when you're gone?"

"M—Morton will miss me," Olive stammered.

"Morton would have gone with anyone who let him out of that painting." The voice chuckled mirthlessly. "If he had had a choice, it wouldn't have been you."

"The cats . . ." whispered Olive.

"Ah, the cats. The cats just want to be rid of me, to be quite frank," said the voice, which now seemed to be coming from behind Olive's knees. "Once all of this is over, they'll forget about you more quickly than your old schoolmates have."

Olive could barely breathe. "How do you know about that?" Her voice was a tiny wisp in the icy air.

The voice laughed again. "At all of those schools you've left, no one is saying, 'Where is that Olive Dunwoody?' They forgot your name long ago. Some of them never knew it at all. Most haven't even noticed that you're gone."

The darkness was getting inside of her. Olive could feel it. It had seeped in through her eyes, and her ears, and her skin, and now everything inside of her was dark. The world was just as dark and empty, full of holes left by people she didn't even know. Darkness was all that was left. Darkness, and some tiny thing she was trying to remember, but it kept slipping away from her grasp, like a floating dandelion seed.

"Ask yourself, Olive: Who would notice? Who would care if you just . . . disappeared?"

A small, warm breeze stirred the frigid air, and Olive knew the tiny attic window was open. "What lovely moonlight," said the voice. "Just enough light to look at these paintings. They are all still there, you know. Come and see." Olive heard the soft clack of canvases falling against each other, and knew that the thing—Aldous McMartin, or whatever it was—was flipping through the stack of paintings where she had once found Baltus. "I would even let you choose, Olive. You can decide for yourself which painting you would like to be inside. Or I could paint something new, especially for you." The voice dropped to a whisper. "You've already imagined it, haven't you, Olive? Sometimes you would rather be in a painting than face the real world, wouldn't you?"

Olive didn't answer. Couldn't answer. But way down in the farthest, darkest corner of her mind, a tiny voice whispered *Yes.*

Air like the blast from an open freezer settled on her face. Olive closed her eyes, letting the darkness come closer. It pushed the floating dandelion seed out of her reach. Maybe she should stop fighting, stop trying to remember.

The frost on her eyelashes was turning to heavy crystals of ice. Her clothes were like stones, solid and heavy. She felt so sleepy. The darkness inside her eyelids was much warmer and friendlier than the darkness in the attic. She could rest. She could just go to sleep, and it would all be over.

"Very well. I will decide for you," the voice whispered in her ear. It was almost gentle, like someone tucking her into bed at night. "Then you will truly belong here, in this house, forever. And no one will ever make you feel out of place again." The words wrapped around Olive, warm and heavy. They pulled her down toward the bottom of the darkness. "Go to sleep, Olive. You won't need to feel a thing. No more fear. No more loneliness. Nothing at all."

The last wisps of the world faded away. Olive felt as numb as her toes. Numb to cold, to fear, to everything. Her heart was one big empty room, and its emptiness echoed with the things that were missing. She had never noticed how much she had been keeping in there until it was all gone.

In that big blank darkness, the thing she had been trying to catch, the thing that had been floating through her mind like a dandelion seed, suddenly came to rest. And it wasn't a dandelion seed at all. It was a tiny, flickering light—the light from a candle your mother hands you. The light of a flashlight against a dark sky.

Olive could almost feel the hands on top of hers: her mother's, her father's, Morton's small warm palm, the fur-tufted paws of three cats. They were all there, inside of her, as she pushed the button on the camping lantern.

The sudden brilliance of fluorescent light exploded the darkness. The light was reflected by the ring of mirrors that Olive had moved into place, its beams multiplying, glancing in all directions, building a cage of brightness around Olive and the thing that stood next to her. Squinting, Olive could just make out the figure from Mr. McMartin's self-portrait—something dark, gaunt, and twisted, something barely human—trapped inside the circle of light. In the shadow that should have been its face, Olive could see two spots reflecting the light—two eyes that looked right into hers. But he couldn't scare her anymore. The light was erasing Aldous McMartin. Brightness ate away his

feet, his legs, his long, knobby fingers, his skeletal jaw. When only a mouth and eyes were left, he let out a roar that echoed inside the attic, shaking the dust from the walls, rattling out through the old gray stones. And then every trace of him was gone.

OLIVE BLINKED, LETTING her aching eyes adjust.

The attic was quiet. It was not the ominous quiet that tells you something is sneaking up behind you, but a peaceful quiet—the kind of quiet that makes you want to curl up and sleep. There were still shadows in the corners, of course, but they thinned and shifted harmlessly as Olive stood up, lifting the lantern. She could feel the air growing warmer.

With the lantern in one hand, Olive stumbled exhaustedly down the attic stairs. The door swung open on the first try. The lantern's bright beams fell over Morton and the cats, who huddled together in the entryway, all of them squinting into the light. For a moment, no one moved.

"Olive?" Morton whispered.

Olive took a deep breath. "He's gone."

Horatio and Leopold let out yowls of joy. Morton hopped up and down while holding on to Olive's arm, his round white head bobbing like a helium balloon on a string. Harvey rocketed from wall to wall above them, whooping, "Youdidityoudidityoudidit!" between fits of laughter.

Leopold was the first to collect himself. "Miss," he proclaimed, "your household thanks you. Your courage and cunning in battle have—" But here Leopold was interrupted by Harvey landing on his head.

Horatio gazed up at Olive as Leopold and Harvey rolled through the picture frame and into the pink room in a hissing, chortling ball. Then Horatio smiled. And it was an actual smile, without a trace of sarcasm in it. "I can't believe it," he said. "You did it. You really did it." Olive reached down to scratch Horatio gently between the ears.

Morton threw his spindly arms around Olive's ribs, still jumping up and down. "I'm going to tell everybody on the whole street about you!"

Looking down at his tufty head, Olive felt her smile waver. A lump began to form in her throat, but a stubborn yawn pushed it away. "Let's go get some sleep," she said.

Olive grabbed Horatio's tail and held on to Morton. The three of them trooped out into the hallway, where all the paintings were back in their frames, and all the lights had turned back on.

They stopped in front of the painting of Linden Street. The picture was different now. The sky was a softer, warmer shade of dusk, and a few stars twinkled at the edge of the frame. The mist that had smothered the field had thinned to a few decorative wisps. In the distant houses, Olive spotted the glimmer of cheerful lights.

Olive cleared her throat. "I guess—I guess this didn't really help you," she said, looking everywhere but at Morton. "I mean, it won't help you get back home. To your *real* home."

Morton was quiet.

Olive forced out the next words. "Morton, I don't know how to help you. I can't make what happened to you *not* have happened."

"I know," Morton said softly.

"I'll keep trying, though," Olive promised. "Maybe someday . . ." She trailed off. There were no words to finish that sentence.

"Olive?" said Morton. "That light is hurting me."

"Oh. I'm sorry." Olive turned off the camping lantern. Morton cautiously rubbed his arm, where it had been closest to the bright light. For a moment, neither of them spoke.

"I'll come visit you, though," Olive said at last. "I

mean, if you want me to. And if the cats will bring me."

Horatio rolled his eyes in a beleaguered sort of way, then nodded.

"I want you to," said Morton. "That would be fun."

"Morton," said Olive, leaning her forehead against the wall so that Morton couldn't see it if she started to cry, "I'm sorry."

Morton shrugged. "It's all right," he said, trying very hard to smooth the quaver out of his voice. "Maybe . . ." Morton blinked hard. "Maybe it will be different now. In there."

"Out here, too," said Olive. They looked at each other for a moment before Olive turned away.

"Leopold, would you help Morton get home?" Olive called as the yowling ball of cats rolled back into the hall. Leopold extracted himself from Harvey's grip, gave Olive a salute, and offered Morton his tail.

"Godspeed, Sir Pillowcase!" cried Harvey to Morton with a knightly wave as Leopold and Morton slipped through the frame.

Olive let out a deep breath. Then she scuffled into her own bedroom and flopped down next to Hershel in a pile of fluffy pillows and soft, warm blankets. Before she could think another thought, she had fallen asleep.

WE'RE HOME!" CALLED Mr. Dunwoody cheerily from the front door.

Olive looked up from a massive breakfast of hot cocoa, bananas, Mrs. Nivens's cookies, and pink kittens with marshmallows. Mrs. Dunwoody swept down the hall to the kitchen and gave Olive a kiss on the forehead.

"How was the conference?" Olive asked.

"It was illuminating," said Mr. Dunwoody, setting down the suitcases. "We brought you something." With a flourish, he unfolded a T-shirt printed with a chicken and held it up for Olive to see.

"'Why did the chicken cross the Möbius strip?'" Olive read aloud. Mr. Dunwoody turned the shirt around to the back. "'To get to the same side.'"

Mr. Dunwoody beamed. "Do you get it?"

"Kind of," said Olive.

Mrs. Dunwoody patted Olive's shoulder patiently. "How was everything here while we were away?"

"It was fine," said Olive, swallowing a large mouthful of cookies. "The electricity went out for a while."

"Were you all right?"

"Yes." Olive shrugged.

"What a brave girl," said Mrs. Dunwoody. Then she sneezed. "Olive, dear, you are covered in cat hair."

"Oh." Olive glanced at her shirt, which was indeed coated with a thick furze of black, orange, and white cat hair. All three cats had piled themselves on top of her during the night. She had woken with Leopold on her feet, Horatio on her stomach, and Harvey curved over her head like a furry beret. "Actually, there's something I have to tell you . . ." Olive looked up at her parents. "We have three cats."

"What?" said Mrs. Dunwoody.

"Did you buy three cats while we were gone, Olive?" asked Mr. Dunwoody.

"No, they were here before we came." Olive toyed with her mug. "They've been here all along. I don't think we can make them leave."

Mr. Dunwoody nodded, frowning thoughtfully. "It hasn't ever seemed fair to me that animals never get to decide where they would like to live for themselves."

Olive looked up at her parents, making her eyes as pleading as possible. "Can they stay? I'll make sure they don't ever go in the library or your bedroom. They're all very well-behaved." She paused, thinking of Harvey. "Well, *almost* all."

Mr. Dunwoody looked down at Mrs. Dunwoody. "What do you think, sweetheart? The responsibility might be good for Olive. And we have this big house . . ."

Mrs. Dunwoody sniffled. She looked at Olive's hopeful face and sighed. "All right. I'll just have to get an anti-allergy injection, I suppose."

Olive wrapped her parents in an energetic hug, then rushed upstairs to give the cats the news.

Mr. Dunwoody looked mistily down at his wife. "Thank you, dear," he said, lifting her hand and kissing it. "My love for you is a monotonic increasing function of time."

Mrs. Dunwoody sneezed.

Olive, Horatio, Leopold, and Harvey, who was wearing a bedraggled white feather between his ears, stood together in the upstairs hallway.

"Why the feather?" Olive whispered to Horatio.

"Cyrano de Bergerac," Horatio answered dryly.

Olive gazed around at the paintings, which all seemed a bit friendlier than before. All but two, anyway. An empty portrait frame hung in the violet guest room, and the painting of the dark forest now featured a woman with disheveled hair and a very sour expression.

Olive tapped the corner of the frame, and the forest painting swung back and forth on its hook just like any ordinary picture.

"Well, blow me down," said Leopold. "It moved."

Slowly, Olive lifted the heavy picture from the wall. Ms. McMartin didn't move, but she seemed to glare even more pointedly out of the frame.

The four companions carried the painting out into the backyard. Olive lay it on the dewy grass and brought a shovel from the garden shed. Harvey got merrily to work, slinging pawfuls of dirt in all directions. Leopold directed the excavation, and Horatio sat at a short distance, keeping his luxuriant fur clean.

When the hole was several feet wide and deep, Olive wedged the painting soundly inside. Ms. McMartin glared up at them. Olive scooped in the first heap of compost. Soon the painting was completely hidden from sight. When the hole was neatly filled in, the cats walked up and down on the fresh-turned dirt, tamping it down with their round footprints.

"There," said Olive. "The end."

"Well done, miss," said Leopold with a dignified nod. "Victory is ours."

"En garde!" shouted Harvey, pouncing after a grasshopper.

Horatio winked at Olive, then began cleaning the crumbs of dirt from his fur.

Back inside the house, Olive was pouring a glass of milk for herself and three dishes for the cats when

something across the room caught her eye. Olive moved closer to the painting of the three men who had been building a wall. The men had put down their stones and were now seated on the grass, all of them patting a big dark brown mutt. The dog's face wore an expression of tongue-lolling ecstasy.

Olive smiled. Baltus wouldn't be bothering the cats again.

The quiet tapping of computer keys filtered from the library where Mr. and Mrs. Dunwoody were finishing their work for the day. As the sun dipped lower in the sky, the porch swing creaked gently in its nook of ferns and ivy. Olive ran her fingers along the banister that ran up the wide staircase. This was her house now. And she liked it here.

She paused next to the painting of Linden Street. Lights glowed cozily in the distant houses, and a few stars twinkled softly in the twilit sky.

"Good night, Morton," Olive whispered.

Then she headed back down the stairs. There was a lot more to explore.

First, huge thanks to my fabulous agent, Chris Richman, for taking a chance on me and Olive, and for being the pilot fish to my whale shark (or, if he prefers, the grooming bird to my hippo).

Equally huge thanks to Jessica Garrison for her kindness, her wisdom, her humor, and her unflagging encouragement, and to all the wonderful people at Dial—notably copyeditor Regina Castillo, who went through this manuscript with infinite patience and a comb so fine-toothed it would find the tangles on a chinchilla.

To Phil and Andrea Hansen and to Amelia West for the magical naming of cats: thank you, thank you, thank you. You all rock.

I will always be grateful to the staff and students of Stockbridge Schools, Stockbridge, Wisconsin, for their generosity and support.

And finally, to all the Cobians, Swansons, McHargs, Nelsons, and Wests who read this in all its many drafts and phases: I love you, and I am so lucky to have you.

JACQUELINE WEST is obsessed with stories where magic intersects with everyday life—from talking cats, to enchanted eyewear, to paintings as portals to other worlds. What paintings might she sneak into if she got her hands on Olive's old glasses? "I would probably have to go with Salvador Dalí's paintings," she says, "because they would be such amazing worlds to explore. I imagine everything would feel rubbery and slick, sort of like Silly Putty or fried eggs." An award-winning poet, Jacqueline lives with her husband in Red Wing, Minnesota, where she dreams of talking cats, dusty libraries, and many more adventures for Olive and Morton. This is her first book.